Praise for *Ch*

A fast, fun, uplifting read.

    Adair Lara, author of *Naked, Drunk, and Writing*

These oddball "nuns" draw us into the conflicts, chaos, and comedy of their lives. A "prioress" who has lost her God, a newly-clean refugee from Silicon Valley trying to seize power, a pickleball addict, a former coven CEO, and a 90-year-old with visions of the Second Coming swirl around one another until everybody finds her best place in this entertaining and intriguing collage. A dive into the chaos when everybody's holy mask cracks at the same time; a sly look at the cacophony of "consciousness" organizations; and a fast-paced tour of where and how one woman finds her God. Set in San Francisco and Sonoma, this book captivated me and made me think.

    Marsh Rose, author of *Escape Routes* and *Lies and Love in Alaska*

This is a great read with an inspiring message just beneath the surface. Catherine travels a tough spiritual passage, but in the spirit of Rosalind Russell. Mary Margaret may be 90 and intermittently off the rails, but we live inside her zeal as she draws media attention for her Facebook posts about her visions. We share Teresa's excitement as she latches onto Mary Margaret's PR star and plots to shatter the "convent's" peace and serenity by hawking it as a Consciousness Circuit stopover. It seems impossible that everyone will get what she wants, but somehow they do. And we do, too. Some fun, some reflection, and a new look at personal freedom.

    Ruth C. Chambers, author of *The Receding Tide*

CHAOS
at the
NO NAME
CONVENT

A Novel

Carol Costello

New Horizons Library

San Francisco, California

Copyright © 2023 by **Carol Costello**

All rights reserved. No part of this publication may be reproduced, distributed or transmitted in any form or by any means, without prior written permission.

New Horizons Library
825 LaPlaya #426
San Francisco, CA 94121
www.carolcostello.net

Publisher's Note: This is a work of fiction. Names, characters, places, and incidents are a product of the author's imagination. Locales and public names are sometimes used for atmospheric purposes. Any resemblance to actual people, living or dead, or to businesses, companies, events, institutions, or locales is completely coincidental.

Chaos at the No Name Convent: A Novel / Carol Costello-- 1st ed.
ISBN: 978-0-9836837-9-7

Book Layout © 2017 BookDesignTemplates.com

Cover photo @ kevers | Depositphotos.com

Cover design by Cathi Stevenson

CONTENTS

THE IMPOSTER PRIORESS 1
THE CANDY APPLE PHONE 15
A DISQUIETING EVENING AT HOME 33
THE IT WIZARD 53
NUN ON THE LOOSE 63
SILICON VALLEY IN THE HIMALAYAS 77
SPIRITUAL MISDIRECTION 91
A WALK IN THE PARK 101
THE UNHOLY ALLIANCE 111
SCRAMBLE 123
RUNAWAY 131
HOME ALONE 139
READY FOR MY CLOSE-UP 155
TIPPING POINT 173
SMACKDOWN IN THE CHAPEL 183
WAKING UP 191
THE NEW LAND 209
KINTSUGI 221

CHAPTER ONE

THE IMPOSTER PRIORESS

Sister Catherine, prioress at the No Name Convent, as it would come to be known, slipped out of her short "power meditation" a bit early. It had not been a great sit, but at least she had made the effort. It would be foolish not to do so, especially now and even if she had to do it at her desk, regrettably indoors on this crisp, sun-splashed fall morning. She drummed her fingers on the polished maple and looked out the window to Golden Gate Park. Monterey cypress, towering redwoods, fluttering eucalyptus. Living splashes of velvety dark greens, amber-tinged ochres, and earthy red-browns against a bright cobalt sky. She longed to run across the street, breathe in those colors, feel the stiff breeze on her face, and let it all take her back to the time when she'd had the only thing that mattered—the time when she had lived absorbed in the Divine and moved gently in that radiant state. The time when life had been real.

Instead, she was stuck here, waiting for the bustling little Sister Teresa, a jittery twenty-something who had been "in tech" but had showed up at their door a year ago in anguished tears, claiming a wild but vague conversion experience and begging to be taken into "this sanctuary of peace." Catherine half smiled at the memory. She had tried to explain to the overwrought Silicon Valley refugee that this was probably not at all the kind of place she was imagining—a silent, incensed, stone-hewn 16th century cloister but with modern plumbing and central heating where nuns cared for the afflicted (herself) and regularly fell to the floor, overcome by visions. They were certainly not that. In fact, their order was probably unique in all the world.

The convent had been founded and endowed ten years earlier by a San Francisco socialite who, months before her death, decided that her time on Earth might have been better spent in silent retreats than at swank Pacific Heights cocktail parties. She was determined to leave behind some sort of spiritual legacy, and seamlessly set up a convent of "wise contemplative women" in a building recently vacated by actual Carmelite nuns—gathering the original twelve from among the meditators, healers, and assorted students and devotees whom she had encountered on her forays into California Consciousness Circuit retreats, workshops, and seminars.

Catherine remembered the evening the socialite had recruited her. After hours of dutifully circulating and making small talk with the St. Francis Hospital Board, she had stopped at the bar to order one last neat Scotch when she felt someone moving toward her from across the room. She looked up to see a woman in a forest green sheath and pearls with startling blue eyes, high cheekbones, and a stylish pageboy expertly streaked to hide the grey. She knew this woman from somewhere. A workshop or seminar? Sierra Club? A past life? They smiled at the same time. The woman leaned an elbow on the bar and offered her hand.

"Leah Sedgewick," she said.

"Catherine Walsh."

"The Public Relations Director."

"How did you know?"

"Let's go see the sunset."

They walked out onto the balcony overlooking Bay and Golden Gate Bridge. The last sliver of a copper-orange sun was sinking into the ocean, surrounded by vibrant lines of tangerine, magenta, and gold. A breeze came up as lights flickered on around the city.

"Where are you from?" Leah asked. It was a common conversation-starter since hardly anyone was actually from San Francisco, but Catherine felt that the question wasn't just about geography. Before long, they were comparing histories and discovering some common stops on the spiritual path. Encouraged by the Scotch, which was not her first of the evening, and the glimmer of a new friendship, Catherine shared about her glorious time in India and her attempts to recapture that blissful state after coming back. Leah shared her plan to buy the convent as a sacred gathering place for women, and they started brainstorming. An hour later, Leah offered her the prioress job and Catherine jumped at it.

Outwardly, the newly-minted "nuns" modeled themselves on traditional convent life, even to wearing long, belted aubergine robes that were habit-ish but also somewhat stylish—a treat for those among them who, as Catholic children, had dreamed of being cloistered Carmelites like St. Teresa of Avila. It did no harm to play with the nostalgic baubles of the Old Church, Catherine had decided, even if they had their own way of doing things and certainly no connection to Catholicism.

Their *Credo* was the Perennial Philosophy of the mystics. Catherine picked up the elegant little ecru card on the corner of her desk and read:

OUR CREDO

We come together in the hope of grace, the love of Truth, and the commitment to living as our authentic Self—the infinite One, the Source that creates and sustains all that is. Our purpose is to deepen our experience of that Essence, and to embrace the love, joy, peace, and freedom at its heart.

Catherine had never doubted the truth of those words, and that made her current state all the more distressing. Worse, that state had to be kept secret from the others. She had only recently been able to name it herself, and was still struggling to accept it. She had lost her God. Without thinking, she flicked the little *Credo* card across her desk. Then quickly retrieved it and placed it carefully back on the corner, lest Teresa suspect that anything was amiss.

Teresa had been undeterred that foggy night when she first arrived. She kept insisting that she had been "called" to them and would do whatever it took to stay. Her determination had impressed Catherine, although she would have bet money that Teresa had never had a direct encounter with the Divine. She had, however, restructured their household task schedule in quite an efficient way, organized outings to a number of interesting Contemplative Outreach events, and secured a few freelance IT jobs to bolster the convent's finances.

Teresa was a firebrand, and Catherine hadn't decided whether that was good or bad. The prioress had not lived her whole life in a convent and sensed that Teresa had done more than her share of illicit substances—probably uppers of some stripe—but the younger woman had not responded to her gentle probing about drugs. In any case, Teresa appeared to have stayed clean since coming to them, without much help as far as Catherine could see, and that counted for something. But then there was the kale. On days when Teresa was assigned to cook, she often built entire meals around kale, even after Catherine had referred half-jokingly to "beyond the pale kale" and asked whether spinach might be a softer, gentler alternative to the spiny and, in Catherine's mind, aggressive little vegetable.

Teresa was always pestering her for more responsibility. A month earlier Catherine had finally broken down and turned over the convent's finances to her. Teresa had seized Catherine's hand-written accounts and shoveled everything into QuickBooks. Catherine was taken aback to see all the numbers lined up so systematically, so dryly, with no fudging or question marks or notes of explanation. Giving Teresa the books might have been a mistake, but she wanted to find out more about the little techie, to see how she navigated a bit of uncertainty and perhaps even a few of the convent's smaller secrets.

A rap on the door.

"Come."

Teresa whirled in clutching a laptop to her chest, her robe flaring slightly as she ended the pirouette with a half bow.

Catherine waved away the bow. "Don't do that."

"But Mother…"

"Catherine. Please. Sit."

Teresa swept into a chair and folded her hands on top of the laptop.

"You have something to show me?"

"Well, Mo...Catherine," Teresa shifted in the chair, glanced up at Catherine and opened the computer. "I've found some oddities."

Catherine motioned for her to bring the laptop behind the desk so they could look at the screen together. Teresa rattled off a barrage numbers, pointed here, pointed there, and finally indicated the bottom line. The socialite's endowment, plus what Teresa took in from her IT freelancing, added up to less than their monthly expenses. But some mysterious money seemed to be flowing into the account at random intervals, so that they were breaking even. Just. But in a few months, without that mysterious extra money, there would be no cushion and they would be living hand to mouth.

"And it looks like this has been going on for some time," Teresa said softly, eyes fixed on the screen. "I'm sure you noticed it when you were doing the books."

"I wouldn't worry about it." Catherine kept her eyes on the screen as well, until she felt Teresa pull away and stand up straight. Then she turned and met the younger woman's startled gaze.

"But where is the extra money coming from?" Teresa asked.

"You're not the only one who makes a private contribution," Catherine said with a thin smile.

Teresa frowned, nodded slowly, then pointed to a number on the screen. "But there's still not enough. Or won't be, soon."

"I see that. Thank you for bringing this to my attention, Sister. I'll see what I can do."

Teresa closed the computer and scurried back to the other side of the desk. She seemed unsure whether to sit, stand, or leave. Catherine picked up a random paper from her desk to indicate "leave" and found that she was staring at the lunch menu from a nearby Chinese takeout place.

"Thank you, Sister."

"But..."

"Let's talk about this next month." Teresa bowed. "Please don't do that. It makes me feel like I'm in one of those old nun movies."

"Ha!" Teresa barked and grinned. She flung open the door and disappeared. Catherine smiled. She liked spunk. Not too much, but some.

She fired up her own computer and logged onto Lacy Dominion's Amazon Author Page, scanned the array of sixteen bodice-rippers and checked their sales numbers. Then she checked the numbers for other books in Lacy's genre. Novels about the high seas were doing well, and those about abductions. "*The Captain's Captive*," she said softly to herself. She would write the first chapter that night.

*

At the stroke of noon, a half hour after releasing Teresa to wonder what might actually be going on with the books, Catherine hurried upstairs to her room at the end of a long corridor dimly lit with bronze sconces. Each woman had a small room with a twin bed, closet, chest of drawers, desk, and shower. She jammed her long dress onto a hanger and plucked from the closet some black tights, a long sleeve turquoise tee, a puffy scarlet vest, and pink and green running shoes. She pulled her long salt-and-cayenne hair back into a scrunchy and took a reassuring glance at the long, slim profile in the mirror. Stuffed her computer, water bottle, phone, wallet, and two power bars into a light daypack and slung it over her shoulder. Made her way down the back stairs to the "hidden" entry and exited into the alley. She was sure people saw them coming and going, but the neighbors were mostly older Asian folks and pretended not to notice the "nuns" traipsing in and out, often in lay clothing.

She crossed the street into Golden Gate Park and gave herself over to the majesty of the redwoods and the windswept beauty of the cypress, the pungent eucalyptus scent, the crystalline air and brilliant blue sky. All the way to the beach today, so it would be six miles out and back. She picked up the pace, added some jogging, and felt life surging through her muscles and veins. Fifty-nine wasn't so bad after all.

On these walks, away from the convent and out among the trees, Catherine could open up her secret and look at it directly, try to figure out what had happened and how to fix it. How had she devolved from the holy prioress whom the others saw wafting through the corridors—an enlightened, self-contained, and radiant leader awash in her connection with the Divine who presided graciously over dinner, sat straight and still in the back of the chapel during evening meditation, and gave spiritual direction to others—to this anxious, confused person who wasn't sure who she was or where she was going, let alone how to get there? And who, no matter what she did, could not seem to find that spark of the Infinite within herself. And had now stooped to play-acting as her former self. That could not be good. The disguise pinched and pulled, but painful as it was, she clung to it because at least it made her feel useful and admired. And in the absence of anything else, she wasn't about to give that up.

The trouble had started several years ago as a brush with Divine Discontent, the sense that her relationship with God had become tenuous, and sometimes even absent. She had shrugged it off at first. Everybody got Divine Discontent from time to time. The connection still hovered around occasionally, and she had reassured herself that if she ever really wanted or needed to get it back, she could do so. But meantime there were Lacy Dominion books to write, a convent to run, and a seemly endless stream of problems that the sisters brought to her. She had convinced herself that without her whole and constant attention, the convent would fall apart. So over time, her to-do list had become her god. She had been too busy to nurture the gift she'd been given—the experience of God pulsing through her, suffusing her, guiding and inspiring her. Then one day, it was gone.

It had definitely been a gift. She had done very little to earn it, and it had been given to her over and over again. When she was six, she had stood in a Chicago public park, staring down at the maple leaf in her hand, and suddenly felt pulled into what seemed like the leaf's soul—something that was huge, vibrantly alive, and unfathomable. And whatever it was, it was the thing that made everything *go!* The gift came again in her thirties at an ashram in Rajasthan, India. She'd been meditating, gazing at the purple OM symbol on the white wall when, without warning, her everyday reality fell away and she was floating in an infinitely loving, conscious field. Everything in the room—the other meditators, the walls, even the ragged edge of a white cotton sheet that covered the floor in front of her—appeared luminous, almost transparent. And that energy wasn't outside of her; she was looking out from inside it. It came again at fifty when they first started the convent. Meeting the socialite had seemed like serendipity, and being offered the prioress job had seemed like divine intervention. In those first years at the convent, she'd had a sense of coming home as the long hours of silence and meditation warmed and softened her enough for the Divine to work its way back into her depths.

She had held the brass ring and lost it. Through laziness, or pride, or fear, or neglect, or simply distraction. She wasn't sure which at this point, but without it, all that was left was a fake prioress writing bodice-rippers to keep the convent afloat and worried sick that she was wasting her life. When she woke up in the dead of night covered in sweat, she was filled with shame.

Enough for today, she told herself. She couldn't think about it anymore. She moved deeper into the park, onto the smaller back trails, and finally came to her favorite eucalyptus tree. She scrambled up its maze of roots and laid both hands flat against its smooth, warm trunk. Then gazed up into its crown, where grey-green and silver crescent leaves danced in the soft breeze and filtered sun. Lower down, six-foot sheets of smooth bark had peeled off and swayed languidly against the trunk, leaving a patchwork of velvety grey, buff, sage, and reddish brown where they had been. She wanted to pray but didn't know what to say, or to whom, so she climbed down slowly from her perch and got back on the trail.

Catherine smelled the ocean, and suddenly there it was—sapphire, bottle green, and a surreal, nearly metallic blue, with frothy waves and whitecaps blowing back on themselves in an offshore wind. She jogged across the Great Highway, put her shoes in her pack, and ran toward the water. The waves splashed up to mid-calf and nearly pulled her off her feet as they swept back out to sea. Delicious.

She waded back to shore, shed her pack, sat down on the sand, and let herself think about running away. It was her favorite fantasy, and she even let herself imagine who might replace her if she started over in Mendocino, Montana, or Mumbai. Pretending that she could replace herself and leave everything behind gave her a reprieve from the anxiety. It acted like a luscious piece of psycho-spiritual chocolate cake and made everything else disappear.

The prioress replacement pickings were slim, it was true. At fifty, Sister Julian was both young enough and old enough. Smart, well-liked, respected, and down to Earth, she could probably manage the convent but showed no interest in doing so. At the moment, Julian was consumed with pickleball, a sport apparently so addictive that it could completely captivate the mind of a woman who had spent twenty years as a contemplative.

There was Sister Mary Pat, who was about Catherine's age and had been a real nun for most of her life. She was a classic. Taught fifth grade for 15 years, high school math for another 8, served the poor and downtrodden during her infrequent sabbaticals, made retreats at the motherhouse, prayed the rosary and took Communion daily, and capped it off with a visit to the Vatican. Then, for reasons that were never entirely clear to Catherine despite her persistent attempts to uncarth them, Mary Pat had basically run away from home. Apparently just left her Missouri convent one night without much—or possibly any—notice and jumped on a train to San Francisco. She had spent several years living in a rundown studio apartment in the Mission District, clerking at the Age of Aquarius bookstore and exploring a number of routes to higher consciousness including meditation, drumming, Buddhism, and magic mushrooms.

Mary Pat had showed up at the convent one afternoon eight years ago, let a bulging backpack slide from her shoulder onto the tile vestibule floor, looked around, and proclaimed, "You folks have got a good thing going here. Where do I bunk?"

Catherine found her inability to pierce Mary Pat's veil of secrecy a bit unnerving, but what could she say? Mary Pat was a real nun, and she was not. Within a few months, Mary Pat had gained fifteen pounds, gotten a modified butch haircut, and taken to eating meatloaf and drinking beer huddled over a TV tray in front of whatever sport was in season. Since meatloaf was not a staple of the convent diet, Mary Pat had secured a "dispensation" to make it for herself once a week and even to pair it with the "obligatory" beer. Despite her age and training as a teacher, Catherine didn't imagine that Mary Pat had it in her to run the convent—especially the sometimes delicate personal aspects of the job—and doubted that Mary Pat would even consider trying.

There was Sister Heather, who had come to them a year ago by way of the Moonpath Wymen's Retreat in rural Sonoma, and who looked as out of place in the aubergine robe as Catherine would have looked dressed up as Lacy Dominion, who was often pictured on the back cover of her bodice-rippers in a black bustier, leather collar, and high black boots. Heather had been the head witch at her coven and so had some executive experience, but Catherine could not shake the memory of a photo Heather had showed her. Seven women stood behind a fire in what looked like a forest, done up in cascades of green and black netted fabric, wielding bells, gongs, small knives, and Himalayan singing bowls. Heather stood at their center in an intricate black veil and dark, heavy eye makeup. Her long, spindly arms held aloft a small smoking cauldron filled with God knew what. It made Catherine think of a large, stunned insect or someone tripping on acid.

Then there was Sister Mary Margaret—not a potential prioress but an increasingly problematic part of the landscape. Mary Margaret was ninety years old, at death's door, and not entirely herself. Catherine wanted a good death for the old woman, who had also been an actual Catholic nun before joining them and now seemed to be drifting back to those days in her unsteady mind, whining about wanting to receive Holy Communion and see "Father" for Confession—two things that would not happen at their convent.

Catherine checked her watch and realized that she needed to get moving. She stood, brushed off the sand, trekked back to the seawall, and hiked to the library. Found a quiet corner and opened her computer. How to begin? Readers liked heroines with Irish names. A moment's thought, then "Captain McCabe burst into Maeve's stateroom and leaned over her. He unsheathed his long, thick pirate's sword and lowered himself onto the bed, pressing..."

The phone rang inside her pack. Julian, who would not be calling—or even away from the pickleball courts—at this time of day unless something was wrong.

"Yes?"

"We can't find Mary Margaret. Where are you?"

"At the library. Did you look in the chapel?"

"First place. She's not here. You'd better come home."

CHAPTER TWO

THE CANDY APPLE PHONE

Julian was dressed for pickleball—red tee, longish black shorts, white tennis shoes and white visor. Catherine stared at the visor, flashing briefly on its likeness to the old-fashioned white wimples that real nuns used to wear. Julian removed it, almost as if she had read Catherine's thoughts, and placed it on the counter next to the toaster. Catherine was glad she had changed into her aubergine robe when she got home. It suggested dignity and order, two qualities she sensed that she would want at her disposal in this situation. Teresa had joined them, at Catherine's request, for the kitchen summit on Mary Margaret.

"I was on my way out," Julian said breathlessly, "and just had a thought to check on her. Not in her room, the chapel, the basement, here, nowhere! She's gone! She could be anywhere!"

"Not *anywhere*," Catherine said calmly. "She can't have gotten far. Who saw her last?"

"Nobody's seen her since breakfast," Julian said.

Teresa tapped on her computer. It annoyed Catherine that Teresa carried the device with her wherever she went. It was like an appendage, and always seemed to deliver bad news. "Oh my God, she's on Facebook!" Teresa said. More tapping, and she swiveled the computer around so that Julian and Catherine could see.

Sister Mary Margaret beamed out at them from the header on her Page—a selfie of an ancient, ecstatic nun smiling broadly, projecting a level of bliss that none of them had ever seen in her. They looked up at one another. "Shit!" Julian whispered.

In the background of the selfie, a grey stone Gothic church. Catherine pointed to it. "That's gotta be St. Dominic's."

"What's she doing there?" Julian asked.

"Probably going to Confession and getting Communion," Catherine said dryly.

Teresa scrolled down. "Look at these posts." The other two leaned in. Another glowing Mary Margaret, this time standing somewhere in the Marina with her arms raised above her head and the Golden Gate Bridge in the background. "Come, follow me. I will give you the glory of God." The next post caught Mary Margaret's rapturous grin high atop some hill—probably Twin Peaks—with one arm outstretched to the San Francisco skyline below. "Stay tuned for God's Voice, livestreaming soon." And another of Mary Margaret looking directly into the camera with an intimate, incandescent smile. "Be still, and know that I am God."

Catherine squinted at the screen. "That's *here*. In the dining room. See?" She pointed to a blurry OM symbol on the wall behind Mary Margaret.

"Jeez," Julian breathed.

"I thought she was supposed to be dying," Teresa said.

Catherine raised her eyebrows and gave Teresa a wry look. "Apparently not. Run over to St. Dominic's and see if she's there."

"But Mo...Catherine, it's almost two miles away. How could she..."

"She apparently has her ways, Sister," Catherine said, indicating the Facebook posts from all over the city. "She probably has a bus pass."

"But where would she get...?" Teresa began.

Julian edged over toward the counter and began examining a frayed thread on her visor. Catherine was at her side in an instant. "No. You didn't," she said under her breath.

Julian's eyes darted around the kitchen, then back to Catherine. "I'm so sorry! I had no idea!" Catherine shook her head and moved back over to the computer. "You didn't happen to get her a cell phone, did you?"

Julian shook her head vigorously. "No! Absolutely not!"

Teresa looked at the floor and mumbled, "I gave her my old Samsung and set her up on T-Mobile. She begged me. Said she wanted to send pictures of flowers to her sister in Indiana. What could I say?"

"You could say no. Or ask me." She shooed Teresa away. "Go. St. Dominic's. Take the car." Teresa seemed relieved to have a mission and darted away to the garage off the kitchen.

"Should we call the cops?" Julian asked. Catherine shook her head.

"If we don't have her by tonight, we'll call. I bet she's at St. Dominic's. It's Catholic, it's old, it smells like the Old Church. Votive candles, incense, the whole nine yards." St. Dominic's was eerily reminiscent of Immaculate Conception, her own childhood church.

Julian turned back to the computer, stared a minute, and grabbed Catherine's arm. "Look at this. I didn't see the comments before." Julian refreshed the page and another tranche of comments fell onto the screen.

"Dear, dear Sister Mary Margaret, you bring God down into our midst."

"My grandson's broken arm is healed! Thank you, Sister!"

"Please, Sister, send the divine live-stream soon."

"I am twenty days sober, thanks to you."

"She's been at this for *three weeks*?!" Catherine asked incredulously. She usually had a much better sense of what was going on in the convent. Julian scrolled down and began counting the comments.

"Thirty-nine. They're all like that. Healings, miracles, visions. It's like she's John the Baptist. Or…"

Catherine held up her hand. "Don't even say it. Sister Mary Margaret is not—I repeat, *not*—the Second Coming of Christ. Did you look for a phone when you were in her room?"

"No."

Catherine nodded toward the stairs, and Julian sprinted away. Catherine picked some red seedless grapes out of the fruit bowl on the counter and popped them slowly, thoughtfully into her mouth. Not only had she missed whatever Mary Margaret was up to, but neither Julian nor Teresa had confided in her about helping the old nun with what was shaping up to be a Quasi Second Coming. They probably hadn't suspected the uses to which Mary Margaret would put the phone and bus pass, or been aware of what the other one was doing, but they should have asked her. She would have to reengage here, contain this Mary Margaret thing, encourage Julian to step up more, and bring Teresa closer into the inner circle. Her mind drifted to what Mary Margaret might have procured from Heather. A ceremonial feather? Exotic incense? Or Mary Pat. A dog-eared St. Joseph's Missal, as a prop to lure in every "fallen away" Catholic over sixty?

Something about Mary Margaret's sudden evangelism made Catherine angry. She knew that was completely inappropriate. Unworthy and venal. But there it was. It wasn't just that the convent routine was disturbed and that their privacy might be threatened; it was deeper, more personal than that. It was jealousy, she realized suddenly. What had Mary Margaret done to deserve downloads from the Divine, while she herself was languishing in the spiritual desert? Even if the downloads were just delusional, Mary Margaret *thought* they were real and obviously got joy from them—which was a lot more than Catherine could say.

Julian rushed in holding at arm's length the old Samsung, nestled in a shimmering candy apple red case.

"Dear Lord." Catherine reached for it and scanned the home screen, then laid it on the counter.

"Why doesn't she have it with her?" Julian asked.

"Good question. Maybe she's not out proselytizing today. Maybe just wandering."

At that moment, a silent shadow moved across the doorway and down the corridor outside the kitchen. Catherine jerked her thumb toward the door and Julian hurried into the hallway, calling, "Sister? Sister Mary Margaret?" Some scuffling, then a muffled, "Come with me, dear."

They appeared in the doorway together, both looking a little guilty. A tableau of truancy, Catherine thought. Rangy Sister Julian, 5'11, with her arm around the diminutive Sister

Mary Margaret, never tall but now stooped and barely 5'. "Look who I found, Sister, our dear Mary Margaret."

The old nun seemed confused for a moment, narrowed her eyes at Julian and turned down the corners of her mouth into a mass of wrinkles. Then suddenly, her face came alive with the same radiance she had displayed on Facebook. Her ancient blue eyes sparkled with wonder and delight. She held her arms above her head and burst into song. "Mine eyes have seen the glory of the coming of the Lord!" Then, as quickly as the glory had come upon her, it disappeared. She lowered her arms, folded her hands at her waist, and fixed Catherine with a knowing look. "Yours will, too. Maybe. We'll see."

"Sister!" Catherine enveloped the little nun in a hug. "We've been worried about you. Where have you been?"

"With my Father." She pointed up toward the ceiling, apparently indicating her Heavenly Father.

Catherine and Julian exchanged looks above her head. Mary Margaret suddenly spotted the candy apple phone on the counter and lunged for it, but Catherine was quicker and snatched up the shiny red treasure before she could reach it.

"My phone! Give it!" Mary Margaret said fiercely and grabbed at the phone with a strength that shocked Catherine. Gnarled fingers closed around it and tried to wrench it out of Catherine's hand. "*Give it!*" Mary Margaret shrieked, and Catherine finally let go. Mary Margaret staggered back a step, but steadied herself and clutched the phone to her chest. "You think you're so smart," she muttered and turned to escape, but Catherine put a hand on her arm.

"Sister," Catherine said gently, slipping her arm firmly around Mary Margaret's shoulder. "Please stay a minute and talk." Mary Margaret looked up suspiciously. "Please!" The vow of obedience dies hard, Catherine thought. Mary Margaret glared at the floor and held the phone behind her back. "Thank you. Now won't you tell us where you've been?"

"I've been to church. Gone to Confession. I'm ready to die."

"Oh, now Sister, you're not going to die today. And thank you for telling us where you were. St. Dominic's?" Mary Margaret nodded. Catherine smiled warmly. "You scared us. How would we get on without you?"

"You'd manage," Mary Margaret said tightly.

"We'd manage. But it wouldn't be the same." Tears appeared in Mary Margaret's eyes. "I'd like you to promise me that you'll tell us where you're going when you leave."

"I must be about my father's business." Mary Margaret wiped away the tears.

"I know, dear, but we need to know where you are. So we can help you if you need anything."

Mary Margaret fidgeted with the phone, stepped back, then forward. Spread her arms and shouted with a strange combination of anger and ecstasy, "I will not need anything! Nothing! I am alive in God's heart! I..."

She tipped to the left, her arms fell to her sides, and her eyes slowly rolled back in her head. Catherine jumped to catch her as she crumpled to the floor. The candy apple phone skittered across the terra cotta tiles, and Julian snagged it just before it disappeared under the fridge. Catherine knelt over Mary Margaret and said quietly to Julian, "Call 911." She heard Julian make the call, and then moments later heard her mutter, apparently to Teresa, "We have her. Come home."

Catherine searched Mary Margaret's withered, ashen face. She touched the pale parchment skin. It was cold and dry, but when she took the ancient veined hand in hers, Mary Margaret's eyes flew open, wide and terrified. She struggled to sit up, but Catherine gently pushed her back.

"Don't move, Sister. You've taken a fall. We've called an ambulance."

Mary Margaret cast her eyes about at Julian, at Catherine, and then proclaimed to some unseen presence over by the fridge, "Awaken leeks!" Catherine pulled back and sat on her heels. She was prepared to deal with a swoon, even a stroke—but not with word-salad-level derangement. "Koosh," Mary Margaret said softly. Then, with a small shake of her head, she seemed to come around.

"Where am I?"

"In the kitchen!" Julian said a little too loudly. "On the floor!" Catherine frowned at Julian—one crazy person was enough—and Julian sat back on her haunches. Mary Margaret looked up at Catherine.

"I passed out?" Catherine nodded. Mary Margaret looked puzzled. "I've never fainted! I think I'm fine now."

"I'm sure you are, but need to get you checked out and make sure you're okay." Mary Margaret lay back, closed her eyes, and quickly opened them again. She looked as if she were about to say something, but glanced at Julian and stopped.

Julian stood and peered over Catherine's shoulder. "How do you feel now, Sister?"

Mary Margaret looked at her suspiciously. "I have a headache." Then, "A little dizzy. Woozy."

Catherine patted her hand. A siren wailed out on the street, and Julian ran to let in the paramedics.

As soon as she was gone, Mary Margaret grabbed both of Catherine's hands in hers. "A vision! I had a vision!"

Catherine nodded. "I want to hear all about it when we get home. After this." She gestured toward four young EMTs—one woman with a blonde ponytail and three very scrubbed-looking young men—pushing their way into the kitchen carrying large cases of equipment, a stretcher, and a fold-down gurney. They swarmed Mary Margaret, slipped the stretcher under her, attached things to her skin, took her blood pressure, listened to her heart, and stabilized her neck and head.

Mary Margaret endured it all with surprising good humor, Catherine thought, offering her arm for the blood pressure and beaming at the youngest male EMT. She put up no resistance and even emitted an excited little "Ooooo" when they picked up the stretcher and placed it on the gurney. Catherine half expected her to throw her arms in the air and start in on the next verse of "The Battle Hymn of the Republic." She was glad Mary Margaret seemed better—at least she had stopped talking about leeks—but she wished the old nun would pick a place to land, mentally, and stay there.

They rolled her out, and the lead EMT turned to Catherine. "Do you want to come with us? St. Mary's?"

"Yes. Will she be okay?"

"We'll see what the docs say, but we didn't find anything."

Julian held out the candy apple phone to Catherine, but Catherine pushed it back.

"You keep it for now. Find out what she's got on there. Get Teresa to help you. I'll get it later. Call you when I know something."

The door to the garage flew open and Teresa burst into the kitchen. Her eyes were red and puffy. "I saw the ambulance!

What's going on? Did she die? Is she okay? Oh my God, it's all my fault." Catherine paused to stare at her. Since Teresa's initial outburst the night she arrived at their doorstep, she had shown little emotion other than a chronic, low-grade anxiety.

"Sister Julian will explain everything." She turned and hurried to catch up with the EMTs.

In the ambulance, Mary Margaret seemed almost fully recovered. Even cheery, Catherine thought. She appeared to be enjoying the adventure and the company of the young EMTs.

"Now who here goes to church?" she demanded as if they were the second graders she had once taught. One of the guys reluctantly raised his hand about three inches and grinned sheepishly. "Aren't you good! I'm sure your mother is very proud." The other three smirked at his discomfort, but were very solicitous with Mary Margaret.

"You feel okay, Sister? Any aches or pains?" the woman with the blonde ponytail asked.

"I feel wonderful," Mary Margaret said. "Wonderful! I had a vis…"

"You just rest, Sister," Catherine interrupted. She did not want them locking Mary Margaret up in a psych ward. Whatever visions or delusions she might be experiencing would be best handled at home without extensive medical records. Mary Margaret was clearly not the frail, doddering old nun Catherine had thought she was, with only half her marbles, nearly bedridden and at death's door. But neither should she be left to her own devices outside of their safe grasp. Catherine could easily imagine Mary Margaret scoring another cell phone and posting to her following from the loony bin. The old nun glared at her but was silent the rest of the trip.

CHAOS AT THE NO NAME CONVENT · 25

In the ER, they swept Mary Margaret away and made Catherine sit in the waiting room. Soon a pale kid with thinning blonde hair who looked about eighteen appeared carrying a tablet and called her name.

"I'm Dr. McPhee," he said. A doctor? Catherine eyed his badge. Oliver McPhee, M.D. She felt 110 years old. "She's doing well. She has a concussion. Probably hit her head on the floor. We're getting a CT to make sure there's no bleed, but everything else looks good. My guess is, the fainting was vasovagal syncope. The heart slows down, blood pressure drops, and they pass out. It's almost always triggered by some stressful event. Was there…?"

Catherine tried to look innocent and shook her head, then said, "I'm not sure…"

He nodded and seemed to be waiting for more information, but Catherine gave him none so he forged on. "At this point I'd say the worst of it is the concussion. She just needs to take it easy for a week or so. She should see her primary, though. Uh, are you family?"

"Yes. Can we take her home?"

"We'd like to keep her for a few hours to make sure she's okay, but you can sit with her when she gets back from the CT."

"Thank you…Doctor." He flashed her a small professional smile and left.

Catherine found a chair in the corner of the waiting room and pulled out her phone. She made a quick call to update Julian, then leaned back to gather her thoughts. Should she have told Dr. McPhee the truth about how she had triggered Mary Margaret's episode? No. No need to relate a story that might prompt questions about Mary Margaret's mental state—or elder abuse. Of course, who knew what she was saying to the CT techs at that very moment?

On the wall opposite Catherine, a motel art print of a small boat with a red-brown sail, tossing on a windswept sea under silver-rimmed grey clouds. About to clear, she wondered, or ready to throw down a storm? She felt as unmoored as that boat, and wished they would all just stay put, keep out of trouble, and let her focus on her own problems. That line of thinking, she knew, hardly reflected the Oneness of All Things—which was still her yardstick for righteousness, however tenuous her own grasp on it might be.

At least she could start unraveling the Mary Margaret mystery over the next couple hours. She would have the old nun to herself, trapped here at St. Mary's while they "kept an eye on her." She could extract a lot of information in that time. But how to do so without triggering another vaso-whatever?

A short, older Latina woman in light blue scrubs appeared and called tentatively, "Sister Catherine?" Catherine stood, noted the gold cross around the woman's neck and smiled. The woman, who no doubt assumed she was a real nun, gave her a little half-bow and walked her back to a treatment area at the far end of the ER. She indicated a chair, gave Catherine another half-bow, and closed the curtain as she left. More lies, Catherine thought. Or at least uncorrected assumptions. What would her nine-year-old self, a star student and runner-up to crown the Virgin Mary as the May Queen in fourth grade, think of a middle-aged fake nun playing on the sympathies of a devout Catholic hospital worker? She prodded that question far, far back in the line of issues to be addressed that day.

Moments later, two burly young men in blue scrubs with hospital badges dangling from their necks appeared with Mary

Margaret, who was now ensconced in a large rolling bed, propped up with pillows and sporting a white hospital gown with a scattering of tiny blue dots.

"Here you go, Sister," said solid, strapping DeShawn. His muscles rippled as he maneuvered the bed into place and braked it. "End of the line. You okay now?" Mary Margaret nodded and beamed. "Okay, you just stay here, Sister. They'll come check on you in a while, okay?"

"Thank you so much, DeShawn. And James."

As they left, James turned, waved at Mary Margaret, and gave her a quick conspiratorial smile.

"How are you?" Catherine asked, thinking that the old nun looked a little dazed, but otherwise pretty good. A bit wild-eyed, but that could be adrenalin. "They said you had a concussion, but that you'd be alright."

"They put me inside a huge machine. Inside!" She paused to make sure Catherine was appropriately impressed. "Others might have found it frightening, but I took it as a test of courage. Of commitment to God's mission! It was exhilarating!" Mary Margaret crooked her finger for Catherine to come closer and whispered, "I have to tell you something."

Catherine leaned forward, relieved that finding out about Mary Margaret's crusade might be easier than she'd expected.

"I know you don't like me sneaking away," Mary Margaret said. "But I'll tell you why..." She looked around the treatment room, seemed distracted by the stacks of bandages, bottles of mysterious liquids, blinking machines, and other medical accoutrements.

"Yes?"

Mary Margaret snapped back. "At Vespers one night last month, in the chapel, something happened to me. I..." She shook her head. "That's not the right word." She paused, and Catherine was afraid she might stop altogether.

"What happened?"

"You won't believe me. You won't like it."

Catherine leaned in again and took her hand. "Try me."

"I was just kneeling there, in the chapel, when BANG!" She slammed her palm on the bed railing. Catherine jumped. "It came over me. I thought it was God, calling me to heaven with a stroke. But it wasn't our God. Not the one I've known since I was a girl! It was the real God! I could see Him...It, maybe...inside the pews, the altar, the flowers, the colors in the windows. He wasn't a man, or an angel. It was... *energy*. Like electricity, but *loving*. A field. We were all suspended in it and—get this—we were all *made* of it. The other sisters, me, everything. *Made* of it! Like we were holograms inside it!" She searched Catherine's face. "Do you understand?!"

More than you know, Catherine thought. The memory was bittersweet.

She nodded, and Mary Margaret pressed on, "Spirit! That's what it was. *Love*. I wasn't looking *at* it. I was looking *out from* it. It was everywhere, with no edges! And then..." Mary Margaret grabbed Catherine's sleeve. "I heard a voice. It said, 'Tell everybody about me, the One you called God!'" She paused, her blue eyes wide, then leaned back onto the pillows, gave Catherine a lopsided grin, and asked, "How do you like *that*? Honestly, thought I'd died and gone to heaven!"

"Is that when you started posting?"

Mary Margaret nodded. "I had to. I'm going to die soon and this is my mission, telling people what God really is." She leaned toward Catherine. "It's my life's work, and I didn't get it until I was ninety!" She stared into space for a moment, then seemed taken up into a righteous anger. "That's what I've been doing, and you can't stop me. I'll run away if you try." She hesitated, then said, "When I fainted today, I had another vision! God told me to keep going, to keep talking and the right words would come out. 'Don't delay!' God said. So you can't stop me!"

Catherine patted her hand. "I believe you," she said softly. Mary Margaret nodded as if to seal some bargain between them, then stared off into space again—either communicating with the deity, downloading more messages, or just plain exhausted. After a few minutes, she fished around in the plastic bag that contained her clothes and belongings, and pulled out her rosary. When she began mouthing the prayers, it was like putting up a "Do Not Disturb" sign.

Catherine leaned back in her chair. The old nun was like a freight train. And a famous, mission-fulfilling Mary Margaret threatened everything they had built at the convent. She would become the holy sister, the Voice of God, a minor Second Coming. People would flock to the convent, interview her, talk to the other nuns. Their world would be turned upside down. They would lose their anonymity and privacy, their contemplative, peaceful atmosphere. And the real Church would go nuts. Who knew what they would do? Mary Margaret could easily get hurt, accused of blasphemy or even just branded as a dotty old nun. Going public would put everybody at risk. And going public was the name of Mary Margaret's game.

The old nun finished her rosary and looked at Catherine expectantly.

"Well?" she asked, as if Catherine were a child whom she had just admonished and from whom she anticipated an apology.

"I'm not going to stop you. As if I could," Catherine said. "But I want to work with you so that you get what you need without hurting the other sisters. Your mission could put an end to everything we have, so this bears some thought. Some planning. Will you give me a little time to be with it?"

"How much time?"

"Three days. I want you to promise me you won't post for three days, while we figure this out."

Mary Margaret nodded slowly. "You mean while *you* figure it out. Well, hurry up. I'm going to die."

"Are you actually sick, like you said the doctors told you, or was that just part of the nutty old nun disguise?"

"I'm not too sick, but I'm going to die." Catherine thought of the old Native Americans who decided it was time to die, went up on a hill with a blanket, and did die. "If you don't have a plan in three days, I'm going out on my own."

Catherine nodded. There would be no stopping Mary Margaret; she had to figure out a way to contain her, minimize the damage, and maybe even do some good.

"Do you have my phone?" Mary Margaret demanded suddenly.

"I'd like to keep it until we have a plan."

"You don't trust me."

"Not entirely. I feel your zeal."

Mary Margaret studied her for a moment. "I don't like you keeping my phone, but I will bend rather than break," she said. "I will withdraw into myself until your plan emerges. I will meditate and gather strength."

"Good. And don't use Teresa or Julian as your co-conspirators anymore. It's not fair to them."

Mary Margaret was silent for a moment. "Thank you for hearing me. I will withdraw now." And with that, she leaned back against the pillows, folded her hands over her chest, and closed her eyes.

Catherine stared at those veined, wrinkled hands for a moment, then took out her phone and texted Julian another update. How to build a strategy around someone who was rarely in the same place, mentally or emotionally, from moment to moment?

CHAPTER THREE

A DISQUIETING EVENING AT HOME

At dinner that night, Mary Margaret was hailed as a returning heroine. Sister Gemma tacked a little addendum onto the grace: "And Holy God, please bless our dear Sister Mary Margaret for her courage and forbearance under difficult circumstances." A few women glanced surreptitiously at Catherine, sitting at the head of the table. The story of the kitchen confrontation and cell phone struggle had apparently worked its way through the convent grapevine.

They all seemed to be fussing with their water glasses and napkins, or otherwise looking down at the table. All except Mary Pat, who stared directly at Catherine with a mischievous grin, as if she rather admired a nun who started a semi-cage-fight in the convent kitchen. Catherine rarely knew what Mary Pat was thinking, but in that moment it seemed clear that she approved of the scuffle and considered it at least as entertaining as professional football or smashmouth basketball.

Teresa brought in the entrée, spinach and cheddar souffle with a side of steamed asparagus, assisted by little Sister

Jeanne, who seemed to live in the kitchen. Catherine began serving up each of the twelve plates and passing them down the table.

Mary Pat had looked crestfallen when she spotted the vegetarian souffle and murmured rather loudly to Sister Heather on her left, "I always keep some beef jerky in my room. People die without protein."

Julian nodded enthusiastically from across the table. "Chicken!" she opined. "Protein without the fat or calories!"

Mary Pat gave her a withering look and drew a hand across her large, round stomach. She turned back to Heather and asked rather gruffly, "What do witches eat?"

Heather adopted her priestess-in-the-forest air and looked down her nose at Mary Pat with the same haughty expression that Catherine had seen in the coven photo with the black netting and smoking cauldron. Mary Pat's tone had been a bit brusque, Catherine thought, but the laser-like gaze with which Heather now pierced Mary Pat, then Julian, seemed a bit like the evil eye. Heather's irises took on a grey, almost translucent quality and Catherine wondered if she might actually have some witchy power. "Those who follow the Wiccan path," Heather said archly, "only eat eye of newt on Fridays." Then she followed the sarcasm with a dismissive, "The goddess doesn't care what we eat. Pizza, doughnuts, fruit, whatever." She glanced across at Julian. "And chicken...cooked!"

Catherine could not remember ever hearing a dissonant note at the dinner table. Had something been unleashed by Mary Margaret's swoon and trip to the hospital? Or by her unnerving Facebook presence, which had no doubt followed the same information stream through the convent as the kitchen scuffle? Or by how she herself had handled the incident?

Catherine began to load up Mary Margaret's plate, but the old nun spoke from midway down the table, "No side for me, thank you, Sister. I don't eat vegetables that end in vowels." Heads turned, but despite several quizzical looks, only Teresa spoke.

"But Sister, asparagus ends in 's.'"

Mary Margaret eyed her imperiously and said, "Asparagus is the plural. The singular is asparagu." Silent stares for a beat, until Mary Margaret burst into a cackle. No one seemed to know whether she had just made a clever joke, or was having a moment of dementia. Catherine, Julian, and Teresa exchanged glances. An uneasy chuckle spread slowly around the table, and people quickly broke up into smaller conversations.

Halfway through the meal, Catherine summoned Teresa and said in a low voice, "Thank you for switching out the kale for spinach." Teresa smiled. "I'd like to talk with you after dinner." Teresa nodded and returned to her seat at the other end of the table. When the souffle and asparagu were finished, she and Jeanne cleared the table and returned with a massive plate of chocolate chip cookies, still warm from the oven.

"Your favorite, Sister," Teresa said, setting the platter down in front of Mary Margaret.

Mary Margaret examined the cookies, carefully selected one, took a long, luxurious bite, and pronounced them, "Delicious!" A round of applause followed.

*

Catherine retired to her office after dinner with two cookies wrapped in a napkin. Just as she was about to extract one, there was a knock on the door.

"Come!"

Teresa hurried in and sat on the edge of the chair. "How is she, really? What happened, you know, behind the scenes?"

"Nothing. That was it. She had a concussion, the CT showed no bleed, and we waited until they let her go."

"Oh my God, she scared me!"

Catherine waited for more. Teresa fidgeted, looked up at the OM symbol on the wall behind Catherine, then down at her hands. "When Julian said they'd taken her to the hospital, I thought she might be dead. I kind of panicked. I guess I've gotten a little close to her." She glanced up at Catherine. "Setting up the, uh, phone and all. She was really nice to me. I don't have many friends here. It felt good to be appreciated." She looked up quickly. "Not that you don't..."

"Ah." Catherine looked down at her desk, then back at Teresa. This girl was lonely. "Well, I have a special job for you. I want you to be her friend. I want you to look after her, make sure she doesn't go wandering again, let me know if she needs anything."

Teresa hesitated. "You mean, spy on her?"

"A little, but mostly take care of her. She's promised me not to post for three days, and I want you to make sure she doesn't. I'm going to keep her phone, and I'm sure you won't let her use yours. Even if she starts talking about the pictures of flowers and her sister in Indiana. Get to know her better. Make it fun."

Teresa squirmed and glanced up with a defiant look that Catherine had never seen. Then looked at the floor again. Clearly, she did not like her new assignment. Catherine had become very comfortable with silence, but knew that Teresa would not be able to tolerate it for long. Several seconds passed before the dam burst.

"She's just a sweet old nun. I think she really believes God has a mission for her. I bet she does a jailbreak if you try to stop her. I mean, she knows how to get around the city. Right? Short of locking her in her room or drugging her, I don't know how to contain her." Catherine reflected that Teresa seemed to know a great deal about Mary Margaret's state of mind. For the first time, she wondered how the old nun had learned to use Facebook.

"I see. And what do you think about her mission?"

"What?"

Catherine rolled her eyes. "Do you think God has chosen her for a special mission?"

Teresa appeared to be considering this. Had she not done so before? Catherine told herself not to be so judgmental and impatient. Teresa looked at her hands in her lap.

"I don't know. I don't know much about God, really." She glanced up at Catherine. "I'm trying to learn. I *want* to know."

"If you were me, what would you do?" Catherine asked. Teresa shifted in the chair. "Imagine you're in my position, wanting to maintain our privacy, and wanting to protect Mary Margaret from whatever might be out there, and not..." she paused, then decided to risk it, "and not bring the Church down on us. What would you do?"

"I'm not you. I couldn't..."

"Pretend. What would you do?"

Teresa cocked her head to one side, looked at the ceiling, glanced at the bookshelf, and finally returned to Catherine. "I'd get someone to keep an eye on her so she didn't run off, someone who would also gather information for me..." She smiled wryly, then, "I'd spend time with Mary Margaret myself, listen to her, make her feel heard, gently bring her around to seeing that it would be a bad idea." She paused again. "I don't think I'd give her permission to launch a full-blown social media campaign as a messenger from God." She paused again. "Even if she is that."

"Why not?"

"Too dangerous for her, and for us. Especially about the Church. They'd put us out of business. And," she continued *sotto voce*, "they have assassins, right?"

Catherine was taken aback. She'd had some dark thoughts about the Church, but even she had not gone there. She leaned forward with an expression of genuine concern. "Oh, I don't think they'd go *that* far." Teresa looked unconvinced. "Truly. I don't." She leaned back and said matter-of-factly, "They don't own us."

"They'd find a way," Teresa said with surprising certainty.

"Hm. Well, hopefully it won't come to that." She gave Teresa a this-meeting-is-over smile and said, "Thank you for your insights, Sister. They're very valuable."

Teresa should have stood to leave at that point, Catherine thought, but she didn't. Instead, she seemed panicky.

"What if she doesn't like me breathing down her neck?"

"I'm confident you'll find a way to get your job done and also make it pleasant for both of you."

"But I'm just..."

"You're a very resourceful young woman, and I'm sure you'll grow into whatever is before you."

"Ah," Teresa said. Catherine realized, with a small smile, that this was exactly how she would have responded to that statement. It had not escaped her attention that Teresa sometimes tried to communicate in the same wry, arch way that she occasionally adopted. Teresa smiled sheepishly. She'd had the same thought, Catherine realized.

"You see?" Catherine said. "You're getting the hang of it already. Now go find out if she needs anything tonight. Take her some extra cookies. Jeanne can do the dishes. And let's you and I touch base after chapel every morning."

"Yes…Catherine."

Teresa finally rose to leave, but turned just before opening the door. "Have you just done with me what I suggested you do with her?" Catherine put down the paper she had picked up. "Made me feel heard, befriended, appreciated, trusted, and convinced I should do what you want?"

"As I have always said, Teresa, you are a very bright young woman."

Teresa nodded, smiled, and was gone.

She *did* like Teresa, and did trust her. Kind of. Catherine returned her attention to the cookies, and picked the one with the most chocolate chips. Slowly, thoughtfully, she started eating around the little morsels until all that was left were the chips, dusted with a thin coating of cookie. Then she gave herself over to the glory of the chocolate, finished off the chips in three bites, and headed upstairs to find Gemma.

*

Catherine wasn't exactly sure why she wanted to see Gemma, but over dinner she'd had an unexpected urge to reach out to the serene, beautiful, slightly aloof nun sitting to her right. Gemma appeared to carry the Divine in her every thought and step, and to be infused with something that now seemed beyond Catherine's reach. She stayed a little distant from the other nuns, focused on meditation and some monks in Tibet who prayed constantly for world peace. Catherine had always thought it best to let her glide along in her own mystical path, and gave her a wide berth. But now, it seemed right to reach out to her. Maybe she just wanted another perspective on the Mary Margaret situation. Certainly, that was a good enough excuse for the visit.

Climbing the stairs to the second floor, Catherine realized she had never actually been in Gemma's room. She remembered Gemma's entrance interview six years earlier. She'd caught herself holding her breathe as the slim, auburn-haired woman only slightly younger than herself told a story that was not unlike Catherine's own, but that had a different ending. A better ending.

A former pharmaceutical sales associate, Gemma had walked into her boss's office one day and quit, leaving behind a summary of her grievances and a list of prosecutable offenses that she had witnessed while at the company. Copies to her attorney, should the company disturb her in any way. She had sold her belongings and headed for an ashram in New Delhi, where she had "sat" almost constantly for five years. One morning at the 4:00 AM meditation, she had suddenly felt like she was suspended in the air a foot above her mat, enveloped in a vortex of light, alive in the past, present, and future, aware that human goings-on were merely the creative fantasy of the Divine, conscious light at the center of everything.

She had never fully returned from that experience. She'd come back to Oregon and lived off the land in a commune for a while—bee-keeping and bread-making—but found it boring after the heady ashram life in India or, frankly, even the life of a pharmaceutical sales associate. She moved to Portland and taught meditation but had not found students willing to question the reality of their everyday lives and identities, and finally heard about the San Francisco convent through the meditation gossip circuit. Since coming to them, Gemma had been pleasant, done whatever was asked of her, but spent a lot of time in her room and communicated mostly with the Tibetan monks.

Catherine knocked on Gemma's door. There was a long pause, then a tentative "Yes?"

"It's Catherine. May I come in?"

The door opened slowly and Catherine stepped into a little slice of India. Votive candles flickered on the desk, which had been draped in purple silk and turned into an altar featuring a statue of Shiva dancing in a circle of flames. Incense curled up from the window sill, and a wall panel depicted Krishna in a verdant garden, playing his flute. A garnet and dark green batik spread covered the bed. The desk chair had been pushed to the side, replaced with large pillows scattered across the floor. Catherine eyed them dubiously, and was relieved when Gemma gestured toward the bed.

"Sit. Please."

Catherine suddenly felt like a new novice having her first interview with the Mother Superior. She never knew quite how to speak to this strange person, whose connection to mundane physical reality seemed so tenuous—and yet who seemed so at home with herself and at peace with everything around her.

"I hope I'm not disturbing you," she began. Gemma sat next to her on the bed, her wide green eyes fixed on Catherine in a way that was...neutral, Catherine decided. Unaffected by her presence. Very few people looked at her that way. Gemma's skin had a glow that she envied. No longer young, but somehow radiant. Alive. Someday, not today, she would have to find out what kind of moisturizer Gemma used.

"Not at all." Gemma folded her hands in her lap and seemed comfortable with the silence. Okay, Catherine thought, two can play that game—then caught herself in the childish competition, took a breath, and began speaking in what she hoped was a friendly, casual way.

"I'd like your advice on something." Gemma raised her eyebrows. She seemed surprised, but rearranged herself on the bed and leaned forward. "Are you aware that Sister Mary Margaret has been having what may be transcendent experiences, visions really, and posting about them on Facebook?"

Gemma looked mystified. "I'm not on Facebook. I only use the phone to keep in touch with the monks in Tibet. I knew Mary Margaret was leaving here during free time, but…"

"She's going all around the city, taking selfies with cryptic captions that sound like we're about to have the Second Coming here at the convent. Starring herself."

"Ha! Sounds like fun." Catherine frowned, but Gemma kept smiling. Catherine opened her phone to Mary Margaret's posts and handed it to Gemma, who read with a small smile playing around her lips.

"I'm concerned, obviously," Catherine said sternly, taking back the phone and ignoring Gemma's amusement. "I don't want her to get hurt, or for us to become public. But I also don't want to quash this thing before we know what it is. Before I do anything, I want to know if she's just delusional or if what she's experiencing is real. Valid." Gemma nodded and went back to that strange, neutral gaze. Catherine turned to face her and relayed everything Mary Margaret had said in the ER about her mission. "What do you think?"

"It sounds like that's really what she experienced."

"I know it's what she experienced—but do you think it's real, or is she imagining it all?" Catherine told herself not to sound so anxious and testy. Something about Gemma's presence made her feel exposed. Self-conscious, even nervous. She could almost feel her composed veneer falling away and the prioress disguise dissolving under Gemma's even gaze.

"What do *you* think?" Gemma asked in a patient, careful way that made Catherine feel patronized. Pissed off. "The experience of being one with everything…You've been there, I think?" Gemma said softly. Her words were so kind, so warm that Catherine felt seen in a way she hadn't been for quite a while. That made her sad. And grateful. And even more pissed off. The emotional control that she usually wielded so effortlessly seemed to have deserted her entirely. Her only recourse was the truth.

"A long time ago," she said, looking down at the bedspread.

"But in Chapel, you sit. You must…"

"I don't sit the way I used to. Don't discipline my mind in the same way." Was there some kind of truth serum in Gemma's incense? She was horrified to her hear herself whine and whimper like that. "I'm afraid I'm farther away from that experience than I'd like to be." She told herself to stop talking, but her mouth kept going. "It was easy when I was in India, but I'm having some unsteadiness just now, a little slowness in getting to that connection." She hoped she didn't sound as pathetic as she felt. As bereaved.

She looked away and scanned the room. Why did Shiva have four arms? There must be a reason, but she couldn't remember it. Even under the influence of Gemma's weird spiritual truth serum, she hadn't been completely forthcoming. "A little slowness?" Even those words had cost her some pride. At least now, she was being honest and humble. Surely, that counted for something. Maybe not a no muss, no fuss spiritual fix that would put her back into a glorious connection with the Divine before evening Chapel—but something. Surely!

"What happens when you sit?" Gemma asked matter-of-factly.

"I'm afraid my mind gets very active."

Gemma nodded and asked gently, "How long do you sit each day?"

The anger rose up again. She tried to stuff it down. "You mean, not just resting or thinking or problem-solving, but actually trying to quiet my mind and get to that connection?"

"Yes."

"Maybe...ten minutes," Catherine lied. It was closer to two. Maybe one. Or less. Now she couldn't even tell the truth, and was getting more confused by the minute.

Gemma nodded slightly, glanced at the Shiva statue, then back at Catherine. "That's not enough—as I'm sure you know—especially if you're experiencing a little dip in the road. Have you tried two hour-long sits every day?"

Catherine stared back at her. Two hour-long sits? Prescribed by a bee-keeper? Suddenly, it was all too much. Her meagre reserves of humility were completely exhausted. Frustration flooded into the void. Her instinct was to rise to her feet, lean over Gemma and ask her if she'd ever tried to sustain a meaningful connection with the Divine and at the same time run a convent, especially one with a crazy old nun who thought she was Jesus and a fly-by-night former techie with hungry eyes who was her co-conspirator. And also write one bodice-ripper after another just to keep food on the table? Instead, she finally managed a prioress smile—authoritative but gracious, accommodating—rose to her feet, and said pleasantly, "I'll try that. Thank you, Sister."

Gemma tilted her head to one side and frowned slightly as Catherine brushed past her into the corridor.

Fucking *sitting*, Catherine thought as she strode briskly down the hall toward Teresa's room. Only then did she realize she'd never gotten an answer from Gemma about Mary Margaret. Instead, she'd let the conversation ricochet from averting the Second Coming to her own spiritual poverty and Gemma's remedial homework. What had possessed her to spill out all that embarrassing, demeaning information? She needed an ego fix, a little time with someone who thought she walked on water. Someone who had trouble shaking the "Mother" title. The Divine be damned, at least for the moment. She needed some Teresa.

*

Catherine rapped on Teresa's door. No response—but from fifteen feet down the corridor in Mary Margaret's room, a burst of muffled laughter. Catherine stepped quietly to that door.

"I know, right?" Teresa squealed as if she were conspiring with a gaggle of her peers. A long silence, then, "There. Go ahead and enter your password there, Sister." Catherine considered breaking up what might be a social media tutorial, but reminded herself that when in doubt about what to do, it was usually best to do nothing. She had, after all, asked Teresa to befriend Mary Margaret. For all she knew, Teresa was helping her log into an addictive game that would consume Mary Margaret's attention to the point that she forgot all about her mission. She would give them both the benefit of the doubt.

Catherine stepped silently to her own room at the end of the corridor, slipped in, and threw herself on the bed. It had been a long day, and it wasn't over. The evening meditation started in ten minutes. She pulled herself up and made her way down to the chapel on the first floor.

She was the first to arrive. The other eleven filed in over the next five minutes, moving slowly over the dark plum carpet and spacing themselves randomly in the wooden pews. They had switched out the Carmelites' altar for a long polished walnut parson's table with a dark green silk runner. On it sat six large ivory beeswax candles, three on either side of a lush arrangement of fresh flowers—pearly hydrangeas, dark pink Stargazer lilies, deep red ginger, and a few birds of paradise. Behind the table was a round stained-glass window that during the day painted the room with splashes of violet, gold, crimson, and emerald. On the walls, abstract fabric wall hangings in muted purple, sea green, mauve, and salmon with touches of vermillion.

Catherine sat in the back, in the last pew where she could make sure everyone was there, but wasn't in anyone's line of sight. To ground herself, she catalogued all the things she had learned that day. Money was running out. Mary Margaret was orchestrating some sort of Second Coming scheme on Facebook. Julian and Teresa were haphazardly conspiring with her. Mary Margaret might not be as sick as she said she was, but she had a mission and would not be stopped. Gemma had the spiritual goods and now knew that she, Catherine, did not.

Again, what had possessed her to reveal that? Maybe she *should* become Gemma's student, mortifying as that prospect was. Maybe she was unconsciously putting herself in the pupil position, in spite of herself. She had to admit, grudgingly, that any good teacher would have given her that assignment—to sit for more extended sessions. And here she was, sitting in the chapel, with nothing better to do. What could it hurt to try? Actually, it could hurt a lot. She might fail, which was one reason she hadn't tried it much lately. But she would do it on her own terms, at her own pace—not for an hour twice a day—because unlike the semi-disembodied Gemma, she had responsibilities to fulfill, promises to keep, and problems to solve.

She shifted in her seat, grateful that the carpet softened the sound of the creaking pew. Hunkered in the back of the chapel, she felt fairly safe. Nobody would know whether or not she reached that high spiritual connection that, in India, they had called *samadhi*. She sat up straight, folded her hands in her lap, closed her eyes, and tried to empty her mind. She had done this before, she told herself. She was good at it. She could make this happen. It would give her the insight and power to solve all the convent's problems. More importantly, it would get her back on track with herself and the reason she was on Earth. And she would be happy.

Very deliberately, she made her mind a blank—and immediately thought about the financial discussion with Teresa. Should she tell the little QuickBookster about the bodice-rippers she wrote to keep the convent afloat? Wait, she could not think about that now. Again, she emptied her mind. Had those hydrangeas looked a little gone? She opened her eyes to check. No, but it would be nice to add some Queen Anne's Lace. Wait! She let go of those thoughts and returned to a quiet mind. How could she keep Mary Margaret tamped down without causing another vaso-whatever and looking like the villain in this piece? Wait…

After forty-five minutes of playing whack-a-mole with her hyperactive thoughts, Catherine was exhausted. She felt completely defeated. Nearly an hour of applying everything she had to an exercise that was the classic antidote to her problem, and nothing. Worse than nothing. Clearly, she was now out of the Divine loop—on her own to do something she knew could not be done on her own, but no longer worthy of the grace that could save her. Her eyes stung. She stopped breathing and fought against the feelings, but two drops fell on her folded hands. Proof of her failure and incompetence. She could not let them see her like this. Could not *be* like this. She focused all of her attention on one of the birds of paradise on the altar. Banished everything else. Surreptitiously wiped the tears from her face—and in a few minutes, felt almost back in control. Humiliation still hovered around her, but she didn't think it showed. At least not much, in the darkened chapel. She let herself take a few shallow breaths, held perfectly still, and waited for the session to be over.

After ten minutes, Sister Jeanne's small bell rang to mark the end of the evening meditation. Little Sister Jeanne, of the small bells and sinks full of suds. She returned Catherine's nod with a reverential bow. Catherine gathered herself, put on her prioress glamor, and led the sisters out of the chapel.

*

Back in her room, she downed a large glass of water. She had just sat in the chapel, crying. Shedding tears. That hadn't happened since she'd come to the convent. The Catherine who lurked beneath the prioress disguise must be in even worse shape than she'd imagined.

She couldn't deal with that now. There was one more stop before she could let herself collapse for the day. Teresa might turn out to be a good spy, but Catherine knew she couldn't manage Mary Margaret entirely by proxy. The old nun needed to know that someone was watching her—someone who could not be pushed around, duped, or cajoled into complicity. Someone who would remember what she had said a few hours earlier and hold her to it. And yet someone who understood her mission and her commitment. It was tricky business. But actually, quite manageable compared to being adrift in Gemma's ethereal vibration or wrestling with her wild mind in the chapel.

She gave Mary Margaret a few minutes to get settled in her room, then tapped on her door. No answer, just some scurrying sounds within. Was the old nun shutting down devices? Had she posted again? Finally, the door cracked open two inches and one of Mary Margaret's large blue eyes appeared in the space. The door closed, and was reopened with a flourish. A glowing Mary Margaret spread her arms wide and proclaimed, "Welcome, Sister. Welcome to my blessed digs."

Catherine entered a room that might have been a museum for the old One, Holy, Catholic, and Apostolic Church. She scanned the array of holy cards, bleeding and/or tortured saint statues, spiritual bouquet greeting cards, rosaries, and other paraphernalia of the Pre-Vatican II 1950s. Then the social and political action posters and songbooks of the desperate-to-berelevant Post-Vatican II 1960s and 70s. Finally, some more contemporary books by Rohr and Keating, who espoused versions of the Perennial Philosophy that All is One. It was like marching through the history of the modern Church. Where was Mary Margaret on this timeline?

"My, you have quite a collection here," Catherine said, gesturing around the room. A blood red glass rosary push-pinned to an ancient cork bulletin board caught her eye. Attached to it with a paper clip was a faded note, written in pencil: *Confirmation. Mother.* "This is beautiful."

"Mmm." Catherine felt Mary Margaret's eyes on her as she looked around the room. She spotted a tripod propped up against the wall. Was Mary Margaret planning to do videos? Had she done them already?

"You've lived through quite a lot."

"I don't care about any of it! It's all ridiculous!"

"But you kept..."

"That was before. This is now. I've just been too busy to get rid of it."

"Ah! May we sit for a minute, Sister?" Mary Margaret pointed Catherine to the desk chair and sat down on the edge of the bed. "I've been thinking about your situation. Our situation. I was hoping you could tell me a little more about the experience you had, and why you need to go public. Many of our great saints were mystics—St. Teresa, Julian of Norwich, Hildegard—and they felt no need to..."

"They didn't have Facebook! Besides, we're still talking about them all these centuries later so don't tell me they hid under a rock."

"Of course. But tell me more about that night when all this came to you."

Mary Margaret let out a loud sigh of exasperation. "I already told you! I saw everything *the way it is*. We are all made of the same stuff. It's conscious. Creative. Fierce! Everything is made of it!" Her eyes darted about the room. "That red rosary! The chair! The raccoons in the park! There is nothing *except* it." Oh my God, Catherine thought, imagining Mary Margaret at a press conference, presenting this version of her revelation to the world. As if she had read Catherine's mind, Mary Margaret said in a low voice, "It's hard to explain in words." With that, she pressed her lips together and was silent for a moment. Then, "I was so happy. If everyone knew how things really are, we would all just love one another." Tears began to roll slowly down her cheeks, and she whispered urgently, "Don't you *see*? People have to *know*."

"I see how important it is." Catherine kept her voice measured. "But..."

"If we see and don't tell everyone, we are *sinners*. We waste what we know. That's a sin!" Mary Margaret frowned, clearly veering away from tears and toward something more rigid and intractable. Catherine's head throbbed. She might be spiritually lazy, but she was not a sinner. She wasn't sure how much more Mary Margaret she could take at that point. "*You* know it!" Mary Margaret cried suddenly, pointing an ancient finger at Catherine. "I know you do! You would be a sinner if you stopped me." Catherine thought the old nun had begun to look like a wizened apple doll. She passed her hand across her forehead and stood.

"As I said at the hospital, I'll need a few days to think about it."

Mary Margaret scowled. "Well, hurry up. You know where to find me. And you don't have to make Teresa chain me to the chair. Or give me opium."

Catherine's eyes widened. "I'm sure she wouldn't do that." How had Mary Margaret known about Teresa's assignment? Did she have some otherworldly power, in addition to a God-given mission? Had Teresa told her?

The old nun smirked. "I wasn't born yesterday!"

Catherine pulled herself up to her full height. "I just wanted to make sure you had everything you need."

"I could use some help with passwords and live streaming. She could help me with that!" Catherine recalled the hushed conversation about passwords that she'd overheard outside Mary Margaret's door.

"I asked her to companion you. Go on walks. Help with laundry. Other chores." Conversations that were circling the drain needed to be ended. She needed to be *away* and put a shaky hand on the doorknob. "Thank you, Sister. This has been very helpful. Let's talk again soon."

"Are you alright?" Mary Margaret asked, narrowing her eyes.

"I'm fine. Thank you."

Catherine took hold of herself, forced a smile, and exited into the corridor. Out in the hall, she drew in a deep breath and let her hand graze the wall on the way back to her room. She felt better once she was safely inside with the door closed. Everything seemed to be lurching out of control. Mary Margaret. Teresa. Even Gemma. It felt like the three of them were all coming at her, each from a different direction.

CHAPTER FOUR

THE IT WIZARD

Teresa plunged her hands into a soapy sink full of breakfast dishes and smiled. Life at the convent had gotten a lot more interesting in the past few days. When she'd first arrived—what a mess she'd been!—she was lower than low. Minutes and steps from living on the street. And cra-*zy*! She'd just wanted a roof over her head, a chance to start over, and some healing from folks who *had* to be good to her. She'd heard rumors about this strange group on Fulton Street and sensed they could steer her in a better direction. A holy direction. No more meth or coke! She'd told them a bogus story about having a vision like St. Paul when he saw the blinding light, fell off his horse, and right away became Christ's launch director—at least that's how she remembered it, sort of—and they'd bought it! Why would they buy something like that from her, and not believe this totally holy old nun who'd been at the God thing forever, especially since Mary Margaret could probably bring them fame and possibly even fortune?

Anyway, convent life was okay. All the meditation was good for her, she supposed, even though most of the time she was just sitting there turning over random thoughts in her mind. The quiet chores, being able to help out with money through her IT gig and now with doing the books, the fun aubergine robes, play-acting at being nuns. And she'd learned some stuff about God. Not much, but some, and that was a killer investment!

She swished her fingers in the warm, sudsy water. The soapy bubbles made her feel pure. Righteous. Freaking *good*. And the strange thing was, the shit had hit the fan at the convent just when she'd started thinking about going back to the tech world in the Valley. The convent was cool, but serenity wasn't really her thing. She couldn't stay here *forever*. Couldn't imagine never having any more sex or money. She was ready to get back into the fast lane. Whenever she saw one of those enormous white double-decker wifi busses cruising silently around the San Francisco streets, picking up techies on their way to work in the Valley, her heart jumped. She could do digital marketing and make gazillions!

Of course, now she might have a chance to do some digital marketing right here! She snickered. Mary Margaret! What a character! Sweet, too, and so far the spy job hadn't involved anything more dangerous than helping the old nun get up onto her doctor's health care portal. Plus, she was doing a favor for Catherine. That girl fascinated her! What was *she* about? She could just sit there, and you felt like she could turn the room upside down and make you do whatever she wanted. She'd be glad to learn some Catherine tricks any day. Being in the inner circle was a trip.

And Gemma. That girl was the real deal. She had God, which was nice but also a little scary. Having God would throw a monkey wrench into anybody's normal life. What if she went back to the Valley and had to think about God, the biggest thing in the universe, and at the same time try to focus on her job? A little God was great, but maybe too much God was dangerous. She wanted just enough God to make her happy and keep her out of trouble, but not so much that it took over her life like it had Gemma's.

Anyway, she thought as she set the last saucepan out to dry, she was in the mix with the big girls now since this Mary Margaret thing—and that put her in a great position to skim off some of Catherine's power, Gemma's holiness, Mary Margaret's...what? Charisma? Flair for drama? Whatever gave this ninety-year-old nun the power to upend the likes of Catherine and—coming soon, she was sure—the whole convent.

Teresa hustled upstairs to change for work, but stopped to knock on Mary Margaret's door.

"Come!"

She poked her head in. "Ready for our walk later this afternoon, Sister?"

Mary Margaret was sitting at the desk, hunched over an oversized phone. She looked up at Teresa in amazement. "I have 136 likes from the Bridge shot!"

Teresa nodded enthusiastically. "Cool!" But wait! Catherine said she had kept Mary Margaret's phone. Teresa stepped slowly into the room and peered over Mary Margaret's shoulder. "Uh, Sister, is that your phone?" Mary Margaret looked up defiantly and clutched the phone to her breast.

"You can't have it! It's not even mine! And I'm not posting!" Teresa found herself suddenly thrust into the role of convent cop. Should she confiscate the phone and risk Mary Margaret's ire? Or let it be, and risk Catherine's more subtle but searing disapproval if Mary Margaret posted again? What would Catherine do in this situation? Steer to the middle ground, and not commit immediately to either path.

"Uh, okay." Teresa paused. "Where did you get the phone?"

Mary Margaret appeared to relax and said with a beatific smile, "Our sweet Sister Jeanne let me borrow hers. Just so I could see my comments." Mary Margaret averted her eyes. "And because I told her my sister in Indiana was very sick and missed my texts." She glanced up at Teresa. "I'm not posting!"

Teresa was not about to get into a wrestling match over the phone, like Catherine had done, and set off another fainting spell—or worse. Instead, she stalled.

"How many likes for the one with the Salesforce building?"

"Only fifty-three," Mary Margaret said glumly. "But that was a week earlier."

"And the Salesforce isn't as glorious as the Golden Gate Bridge," Teresa said thoughtfully, as if she were actually engaged with counting Facebook likes. Mary Margaret nodded. "Well, Sister, you sit tight. I'll be home about 3:00 and we can go for our walk." She paused and deliberately held out her hand. "I can return that to Sister Jeanne for you."

Mary Margaret met her gaze with hooded eyes. A moment passed that seemed to Teresa like about five hours. The old nun curled her hand around the phone, and it disappeared into the folds of her robe.

"No, I'll do it. You don't have to bother," she said.

Teresa kept her hand out, stood up a little straighter, and said, "I know Sister Catherine would want me to run this errand for you." Another long moment passed. Finally, Mary

Margaret placed the phone gingerly on Teresa's outstretched palm.

"Alright, dear." Mary Margaret waved her away. "I'll be here when you get back, talking with my God."

Teresa didn't care that Mary Margaret's reference to God had trumped her own reference to Catherine; she was the one leaving with the phone in her hand. She closed the door behind her and right away started fantasizing about the triumphant meeting with Catherine in which she would present the phone along with a blow-by-blow description of how skillfully she had extracted it from Mary Margaret's grasp. In fact, she should do that right now, before she left for work!

She scampered downstairs to Catherine's office and was surprised to find the door open. Catherine was all hunched over her computer, deeply involved in something. What?! Teresa rapped on the open door and smiled in at Catherine, who closed the computer with one deft movement of her hand.

"Come in!"

"Am I disturbing you?"

Catherine slid the computer to the side of her desk. "Not at all. What's up?"

Teresa held up Jeanne's large phone with an exultant grin. "Jeanne's phone. Mary Margaret had it. I got it back. Without upsetting her."

"Good," Catherine said casually. "Anything else?" Catherine had wanted her to do just this sort of thing, and she had done it. Where were the "Attagirls"? What kind of boss withheld a little positive feedback?

"It wasn't easy!" Teresa said.

Catherine tilted her head to one side and said in slow, measured tones, "I imagine it took some skillful diplomacy.

You did a very good job." Teresa flushed. Catherine was patronizing her, treating her like a child! After a pause in which Teresa constructed, then rejected, several stinging or clever retorts, Catherine finally spoke again. "I imagine you expected this would happen, yes? That she'd find another phone…"

"Uh, no…"

"Ah," Catherine said, drumming her fingers lightly on the desk. "Another lesson learned. Another tool for your toolbox." She smiled pleasantly. "Did she post anything?"

"She said she didn't."

"Did you check?"

Shit! She should have thought of that! Teresa frowned and bent over the phone, checking Mary Margaret's most recent posts. None, thank God.

"Nothing," she said.

"Well, good job, Sister. Keep me posted." Then, with a slight smile, "As it were." Catherine put her hand on the computer as if she were ready to get back to whatever she had been doing, but did not open it. "Could you close the door on your way out, please?"

Teresa nodded and left with what she hoped was some dignity. She found Jeanne in the kitchen and delivered the phone back to her, then walked fast and hard back to her own room. What a pisser that had been! She had longed to slam the door in Catherine's face, but congratulated herself for not having done so. She couldn't wait to get out of there! And by the way, what was on that computer that Catherine didn't want her to see?

She slipped into black yoga pants and a long-sleeved pink tee shirt, grabbed her bike from the convent garage, and headed to the Ananda Spiritual Center, a complex three miles away in the Marina that housed New Age yoga, coaching, psychic, and bodywork practitioners. The building had once been a bank, and was now a rabbit warren of small rented spaces, each decorated to reflect the renter's specialty and disposition. Tibetan bells could be heard chiming from an aura cleanser's cubby in the back next to the stairwell. Patchouli and sandalwood drifted over the bodywork area. The yoga studio was upstairs, with a wall of windows looking out to views of San Francisco Bay and the Golden Gate Bridge. Teresa did IT and bookkeeping for the Ananda Center itself and for several of the individual practitioners who rented there.

Sophie Goldman, a twenty-something with frizzy brown hair and a Valley Girl accent, was the receptionist/ringmaster who answered the phones and kept everyone in line and on schedule. Her no-nonsense attitude made Ananda's less than fully grounded clientele think twice about cancelling appointments, arriving without shirts or shoes, or getting high in the waiting area. And yet, Sophie projected an aura of serenity and muted bliss. She greeted patients, clients, and seekers as they entered with a soothing "Namaste" and offered them a cup of herbal tea. If they complained about their practitioner being late, she bestowed a Buddha smile and returned to her work. One wall of her sage green reception area was covered with an abstract painting of bamboo shoots; the other held a little case of items for sale: mini-Tibetan bells, incense, mala beads, hand-held labyrinths, Himalayan bowls (cushion not included), and other accoutrements of enlightenment.

"Hey, Soph," Teresa said as she lifted her bike through the door.

"Namaste, Terri," Sophie intoned in greeter-to-the-enlightened mode. Teresa grinned. She sometimes teased Sophie about the "Namaste" greeting when they shared kale salad lunches out on the Marina Green. It wasn't as if people were entering a sacred Himalayan cave when they showed up at Ananda, often the worse for wear.

She walked her bike down the hall toward her office and peeked into the chakra massage room. Parvati was changing the soft warm towels on her massage table, wearing dangly Indian earrings, white kurta pajama pants, and a turquoise tunic studded with red, green, and purple rhinestones. "Yo, Terri," she said with a note of anxiety that made Teresa glad that Parvata would not be massaging her chakras that day. "Can you straighten out my Square account? It's all fucked up."

"I'll stop by later." Not for the first time, Teresa wondered exactly how one might go about massaging a chakra—but her curiosity did not run deep enough to risk climbing aboard Parvati's table and submitting to a session.

Her office was down near the end of the hall, between a sound healer who used crystal singing bowls to release internalized trauma and a mercifully silent Reiki practitioner whose hands channeled the subtle energies of the universe to heal any dis-ease, mental or physical. She propped her bike against the wall and flipped on the computer, revealing the financial condition of Ananda, Inc. and of six individual practitioners. Simple stuff, really, and a lot clearer than the convent's books, what with Catherine's mysterious cash infusions and reluctance to discuss their dwindling resources.

She worked for a couple hours, solved Parvati's Square problem (You had to sign *in!* How did people get along in the world without knowing things like this?), and returned to her office for lunch, a crunchy burrito of carrots, tofu, kale, and onions in a sprouted-grain tortilla. She opened Facebook to see what her former techie friends in the Valley were up to, maybe discover or intuit how much they were making, and perhaps even scout some jobs. But first a flip through her own newsfeed: Contemplative Outreach, Forks Over Knives, cycling groups, then...

"*Shit!* Shit, shit, shit!"

She shut down the computer, tossed the rest of her lunch into the composting bin, and grabbed her bike. What was she thinking, leaving Mary Margaret alone?

CHAPTER FIVE

NUN ON THE LOOSE

An hour before Teresa opened her Facebook feed and saw the shocking post, Mary Margaret had been scrolling down her own Facebook feed. The high-and-mighty Catherine might be "holding" her candy apple phone at the moment, and the strange, jumpy girl who knew all about passwords might have commandeered the larger phone that she'd borrowed from sweet, dishwashing little Jeanne—but Mary Margaret had marched right down to the kitchen and gotten it back! Convinced Jeanne that her poor sister in Indiana was now much worse—in fact, had become gravely ill, near death, and needed constant comfort—and the phone was hers again! God would forgive the exaggeration. Mary Margaret flipped the phone over and again examined the back of the case. A very unpleasant picture of Jesus on the cross. Puzzling. Jeanne seemed so sweet, so benign. Mary Margaret would have expected a pastel picture of Jesus as a little child, possibly cuddling a lamb. Oh well, God had made sure she had the phone, and that was all that mattered.

She returned to Facebook, awed by the power she held in her hand. Power for good! When she was a child, there hadn't even been television. Only radio. She had flown on an airplane only once, when her mother died in Minnesota and she'd gone there from the real convent in Indiana where she used to live. When was that convent? Ten years ago? Yes, that was it. How on Earth had she gotten to this place, in San Francisco, with these strange nun-like creatures who were not really nuns? She had lost track of how all that had happened and really, it didn't matter because God was in charge. Didn't matter in the slightest. Besides, she chuckled to herself, those "real" nuns in Indiana probably didn't have smartphones, or smart little ones like the girl who had given her the original candy apple phone. What was her name? She had known it only a minute ago. Tiffany? Tilly? Tallulah? No. Some saint. Teresa! Yes. She must remember that. She must be that one's friend. God wanted it.

So even though she'd had no TV as a child, she could sit here in this small chair in San Francisco and go anywhere in the world. See anything. She tapped in "Taj Mahal" and started a virtual tour, but quickly lost interest and returned to the home page. She could visit other people, too. She tapped in the name of her old Indiana convent and skulked around their website: pictures of the motherhouse with nuns wearing secular clothes that looked like they'd come out of the sale basket at K-Mart, helping little Black children read, praying in a chapel, walking around the grounds on narrow paths amid concrete statues of saints. Boring.

But the best thing about a smartphone was that she could talk to the whole world, and the world could hear her. That's what God wanted—for her to complete her mission.

She closed her eyes and looked for her God. Immediately, white light filled her mind and soul. Wave after wave of bright, delicious love. And then her God surged up softly out of everywhere and flowed into her heart. Her hand went to her breast and tears streamed down her cheeks. "Oh," she murmured. She knew everything there was to know, knew the task that was before her, knew that everyone had to feel what she felt, know what she knew. She could not hide it any longer. Finally, the light receded and she felt herself again in the chair, in her room.

Each time, God's presence was a little stronger, a little clearer about what she must do. She couldn't let a small, unimportant obstacle like Catherine stop her. Who did the prioress think she was, to wreak havoc with God's plan? Mary Margaret would not be deterred. She wiped the tears from her face and snatched up the phone. The others would be busy with their household chores and meditations. Catherine would be clattering away at her computer, as usual. Teresa was away somewhere. It wouldn't take a minute, what she was going to do. It was right across the street. All those trees. God's trees. The trees that could talk without voices.

She peeked out into the corridor. Silent. Empty. She slid along the hallway to the back stairs, descended to the alley, and walked as fast as she could across Fulton to the park. Scanned the trees until a eucalyptus with a double trunk and long, graceful limbs yearning up toward heaven reached out and spoke to her: "I am God, and I am with you now." It had actually said the words! She was just a vessel, a listening vessel. Mary Margaret approached the tree with its huge patches of grey-green bark peeling away from the trunks and a glorious crown of long, narrow, fluttering leaves. She scrambled over a tangle of thick roots that had grown up through the ground and used all her strength to pull herself up so that she stood unsteadily on one of the larger, higher roots. It would make a great shot.

She extended the phone with one arm, braced herself against the trunk with the other, and smiled into the camera. Click! There, she had captured the moment perfectly. She examined the photo. Yes, that was exactly how she felt. Ecstatic. The tree seemed ecstatic, too. And wise. The perfect dual selfie. She posted it to Facebook with the caption. "I am alive! I am with you now! God with you and in you!"

Her task accomplished, Mary Margaret suddenly felt the spirit leave her. As the ecstasy wore off, panic set in. She had promised Catherine she wouldn't post, and she had just posted. She had better get back to her room before anyone discovered she was gone. But as she looked down, she wondered how she had ever climbed up the two feet to her current perch. She stepped one foot down to another root, but her shoe slipped on the damp wood. Her body began to slide out from under her—and kept sliding. She tried to catch herself against the trunk, but the other foot hit something hard and she tumbled down to the ground. Hot pain shot through her wrist, shoulder, and hip. Above her, she saw only stars.

But she did not pass out! Not like last time, in the kitchen. She had to get herself up. She brushed some of the dirt and leaves off her face and robe, and slowly, painfully, got to her feet. The shoulder was skinned, she was sure, and the hip must be bruised but seemed to function. The left wrist was another matter. It felt like something bad had happened there.

She made her way haltingly across Fulton Street and back to her room. Moving very slowly, she washed her face with her right hand only and ran cold water over the left wrist, which made it hurt even more. She collapsed onto the bed for a while, but didn't want to be found like that so pulled herself to her feet. She was rummaging around in a drawer for some aspirin when someone knocked on the door. She stood utterly still, hoping that whoever it was would go away.

"Sister? Are you in there?" It was that nosy little Teresa. She would likely just push into the room if Mary Margaret didn't answer.

"Come! It's not locked!" Mary Margaret had tried to sound cheery, but she could hear the pain and panic in her own voice. The door opened quickly and Teresa barged in. Then froze, stared at the leaves and dirt that still clung to her robe.

"Sister! What have you done?" Teresa reached for the wrist, which was now beginning to swell, but Mary Margaret snatched it away. Pain shot up to her elbow. Teresa stepped back and folded her arms. "You went to the park. You posted that picture. And then I bet you fell and hurt yourself. Am I right?"

Mary Margaret glared at her, but then her lips started to quiver and she gave in to the pain.

"It *hurts*!" she whined.

"We're going to the ER and getting it x-rayed."

"No! Catherine will know!"

"She'll find out anyway, and be even madder if you refused to get it looked at." Mary Margaret considered this. She would much rather go to the ER with Teresa than with Catherine, who would interrogate her again and possibly forbid her to do God's work. God had surely sent Teresa to help. She was part of His plan.

*

Catherine snapped awake. It was light outside, and the clock by her bed said 3:30. She had fallen asleep in the middle of the day. For hours, apparently. That was horrifying, disorienting. She hadn't taken a nap since age two.

But wait. Something had come to her while she was asleep. What was it? The dream still hovered around the edges of her mind, but it was fading quickly. She closed her eyes, pulled on it, and there it was! She was in the park, and spotted a small light in the sky just above the next hill. It crested the hill and surged toward her, unspeakably beautiful. She started running toward it, but suddenly realized that it would burn her alive! She panicked and turned to run the opposite way. Just as the light was about to catch and incinerate her, she woke up.

She forced her breathing to slow down. It didn't take a therapist to figure out that dream! Intimacy with the Divine had simply been too much. Glorious, but overwhelming and absolutely frightening. In the dream, throwing herself into the light would have killed her. Just as, in life, merging with the Divine and thinking of herself as *that* would mean relegating to runner-up, second-place status the everyday Catherine Walsh, the limited human who clung to an individual identity and walked around the Earth trying to make everything go her way. She had traded the Divine experience for the comfort of being a defined, important person—to herself and to others. Better to be *someone* than to be *everything*. *She had pushed the Divine away on purpose!* Not consciously, but in a sneaky, covert way that kept what she'd done a bit hidden. None of this was entirely new news, but somehow the penny hadn't dropped until that moment.

A knock on the door. She pulled herself out of bed and into prioress mode, smoothed the covers back into place, and shoved her hair up into a tortoise shell clip.

"Come." The door swung open slowly and she beheld Mary Margaret standing slightly slumped over, looking forlorn, holding to her chest a hand wrapped in a pale beige elastic bandage. Teresa stood beside her with an arm around her shoulder.

"Good heavens," Catherine said, "Come in here." The two moved slowly, as if in a procession, until they stood before her. "What happened?"

"Sister Mary Margaret took a fall and sprained her wrist," Teresa said. "We had it x-rayed at St. Mary's, and it's just sprained. Not broken." To Catherine, the words seemed measured, careful, almost as if Teresa were in charge and explaining the situation to an underling.

"I see." She turned to Mary Margaret. "How did you fall?"

Mary Margaret started to speak, but Catherine saw Teresa's hand tighten slightly around her shoulder. "We are here to confess, Catherine," Teresa said in that same semi-official tone. "There has been another Facebook post." She held up Jeanne's outsized smartphone, making sure that the grizzly Crucifixion image was facing away from Catherine.

"But I thought..." Catherine decided it was best, for the moment, not to explore how Mary Margaret had acquired yet another phone—or rather, re-acquired that strange big one. She shook her head, grabbed her own phone, and read the post aloud. "'I am alive! I am with you now! God with you and in you!' Goodness. That's quite a statement. Who is with and in whom?"

Teresa and Mary Margaret both looked a little confused, then Teresa said, "I'm sure Sister meant that God is with us, helping us to be loving and merciful. *Forgiving*." She met Catherine's eyes.

"I see." Catherine turned to Mary Margaret and said more gently, "Is that what you meant?"

Mary Margaret straightened and looked up at her. "I did not mean to disobey; I simply followed a higher call. The spirit moved in me."

Catherine motioned for the two of them to sit on the bed, turned the desk chair to face them, and sat. She addressed Teresa first. "If you were someone just sitting in a café, flipping through Facebook, how would you read that?" Teresa was silent. "Might you think that Sister Mary Margaret believed that she was God, and was within everybody?" More silence. Mary Margaret started to speak, but Catherine raised a hand to stop her and again addressed Teresa. "Well?"

"I suppose some people might think that. But…"

Catherine turned to Mary Margaret. "Is that what you meant?"

"God is within everybody, including me!" she declared.

Catherine stared at her. She'd known they would come to this point eventually. Even if Mary Margaret was truly being guided by the Divine, Facebook was an imperfect vehicle for disseminating mystical awareness. It was better suited to braggy photos of fancy luncheon plates, adorable grandchildren, backyard succulent gardens, and cat rescue videos than to brief, punchy come-ons for the Perennial Philosophy of nonduality. How to make Mary Margaret see this? Catherine considered sending Teresa away so she could focus on Mary Margaret and bend her to this realization—but thought better of it. Best to start gathering these two into a little team, get both of them entrained to her so that if and when she figured out how to deal with this, they would be more likely to cooperate. She would probably need Teresa to help execute whatever plan she devised—and anyway, it would be good for Teresa to see how she managed this situation.

Catherine leaned forward, elbows on knees, and took Mary Margaret's good hand. "You're right, Sister. Of course, you're right. I know that. We are all made of God-stuff." Mary Margaret's smile was half beatific, half suspicious. "And of course, everyone should know. My only question is whether this is the most effective way to share it. People have been trying for centuries, millennia to..."

"*I* haven't!" Mary Margaret interrupted. "*I* haven't tried yet."

Catherine glanced at Teresa, who was leaning back on one elbow and looking from one to the other as if she were watching a tennis match, a fascinated observer who had had no real part in the matter. Catherine decided to toss her the ball, and at the same time short-circuit this conversation with Mary Margaret, which was headed toward a bad choice for her: either letting the old nun post, or looking like she was sabotaging humanity's path to enlightenment.

"What do *you* think? Are we all made of God-stuff?" she asked pointedly. Teresa seemed surprised that she would be called upon for an opinion on this subject, and sat up straight on the edge of the bed. She hesitated, looked at Mary Margaret, then Catherine.

"I didn't know people thought that—that they were made of, you know, *God*. That's wild. Do people really *think* that?" She seemed genuinely baffled. Catherine wondered how she had managed to live at the convent for a year and not stumble across the Perennial Philosophy. It was in their *Credo*, for God's sake!

"They do," she said smoothly.

Teresa considered this new information for a moment. "Cool, I guess. But, you know, *out there*. I'm not sure you can just *say* that."

Catherine pointed to Teresa but addressed Mary Margaret. "This is how the person in the café will read what you're saying. That person will be even more baffled than Teresa, but not nearly as kind. And she will not have us there to explain it." Mary Margaret glared at Teresa and leaned away from her.

Catherine stood, signaling that the interview was almost over. Even if she had figured out exactly what to do, these two weren't ready for a plan yet. They needed to calm down, marinate a bit in the growing discomfort of their predicament, integrate the sprained wrist, and stop this crazy shell game with the phones. And she needed more time to think.

"You and I had a deal, Mary Margaret," Catherine said. The old nun rose slowly to her feet and hung her head. "You didn't keep your end of it. I'm sorry you hurt your wrist and I think that's punishment enough, but I don't want you posting again. Or even leaving here alone. Promise?"

"I will not do it unless I am moved again by the spirit."

"Not good enough," Catherine said.

Mary Margaret looked resigned. "I think spirit is through with me for a while."

"Promise?"

"Yes."

"Thank you, Sister. Now where did you get that ridiculous phone?"

"Sister Jeanne."

Catherine turned to Teresa. "*Again?*" Teresa was silent, stared at the floor and nodded. Catherine shook her head. Poor

Jeanne had apparently been pulled into the conspiracy—no doubt unwittingly—not once, but twice. "Take it back to her immediately," she said to Mary Margaret, "and ask her to give you some ice for your wrist."

She made shooing motions with her hands and Mary Margaret turned to go. Teresa started to follow but Catherine laid a hand on her shoulder. "You stay."

Mary Margaret turned back and smiled slyly at Teresa as she moved into the corridor. Catherine closed the door, motioned Teresa back onto the bed, and resumed her seat on the desk chair. She cocked her head to one side without a word and, as she had anticipated, Teresa jumped into the void.

"I know this looks bad, but I can't be with her every minute. I have to go to work." Part defiant, part petulant. "We need the money. I can't sit on top of her all the time."

"What would keep her from posting?"

"Tie her to a chair."

Catherine took a slow, calming breath. "Talk to Jeanne. She's not to give Mary Margaret that phone again under any circumstances." She thought a moment. "Tell Julian as well." Teresa nodded. "And spend more time with Mary Margaret when you *are* here. Get her on our team. Make her feel like if she posts, she's betraying not just me but you. All of us." She stood and Teresa stood with her.

"I'll do my best." At Catherine's raised eyebrows, Teresa said quickly, "Okay. She won't post."

"Good. I'm counting on you." Catherine gave her a minute to get out of the hallway, then changed into "park clothes" and hurried downstairs. It was late afternoon, almost time for dinner, but she needed to clear her head.

*

Catherine crossed Fulton, entered the park at a stand of eucalyptus, and scanned the nearby trees. There it was, the one that Mary Margaret must have used. A closer examination revealed scuff marks on the lower roots and a flattened bed of leaves. She scowled at the tree, then turned and headed west past the DeYoung Museum and Japanese Tea Garden, past the Stow Lake Boathouse into a more hidden area of the park.

This was not her regular route and at every fork, she chose the smaller path until she could no longer see any buildings or landmarks. Finally, she came to a bowl, a depression in the landscape about a quarter-block in diameter surrounded by eucalyptus trees. At the center, some old bricks and charred cinder blocks where there had once been a fire pit, and a rusted, ramshackle picnic table. The amber light of late afternoon cast long shadows over all of it.

She sat down on a tree stump and covered her face with her hands. Banished the tears that wanted to come and pulled out the new insight from her dream. No wonder she kept pushing the Divine away. The everyday tasks on her to-do list at the convent were simpler, more straightforward, and much, much easier than constantly creating and holding a connection with the Divine. An ordinary life was, bottom line, less demanding. Even in times like these, which were frustrating but not overwhelming. A wave of shame swept through her as she realized that without a child's wonder at the soul of a maple leaf or the strict regimen of the ashram, she had gravitated toward the lazier, softer path. Then hidden what she'd done, even from herself. It felt like she kept getting this same insight, or this same family of insights, over and over—but each time she spiraled around to that realization, it went a little deeper into her.

She looked up into the millions of shimmering eucalyptus leaves. *They* didn't have any problems. Why did *they* just get to hang out in the breeze all day, dancing in the sunlight, showing off their silvery gorgeousness? Graceful and elegant. Not like her.

She stood up, turned back toward the trail and looked up to the rim of the bowl. A large russet-colored dog sat very still, staring down at her. She scanned for the dog's human, but saw none. It had a narrow snout, large pointed ears, and rose up into a standing position in a way that was both calm and alert. A coyote! A male, by the coat. Adrenalin coursed through her. Seeing a coyote that close, off-trail and alone, was a little dangerous. And exciting. He had been watching her! Their eyes met for an instant, and she felt like something wild jumped from him into her. He turned slowly and trotted off. She watched him until he disappeared into a thicket, and then jogged back to the convent.

CHAPTER SIX

SILICON VALLEY IN THE HIMALAYAS

Teresa tapped the side of her computer, still stinging from the way Catherine had trapped her into being responsible for Mary Margaret and then not given her kudos for all her good work. That woman had some sort of evil superpower for flipping every conversation to her advantage and always managing to *win*.

She flicked on the computer and opened a folder that she had started a couple months earlier: "Back to the Valley." It contained four files: "Why I Must Get Out of Here," a journal of her increasing skepticism and unhappiness with convent life and her burgeoning frustration with Catherine; "Contacts," friends in Silicon Valley whom she might tap for information or connections; "Ideas" about jobs she might either snag or create, mostly involving digital marketing; and "Résumé," copies of her most recent résumés, which were now at least three years old and hopelessly outdated.

She clicked on "Résumé." Worse than she had expected. She googled around to see what formats people were using now, toured LinkedIn a bit, and spent the next hour trying to spiff up the document. The last year, when she had been at the convent, was a void. What to slot in there? IT consultant and finance manager to major startups? Parvati, the chakra masseuse, was definitely a startup. Sophie, the Ananda receptionist, could probably be persuaded to confirm that Teresa was a finance manager. She guessed that, in Sophie's mind, anyone who could open an Excel spreadsheet was a finance manager. What else? Director of International Marketing for top corporations? At Sophie's request, Teresa had helped Raj Singh, the Indian Ayurvedic healer, put a shopping cart on his website. Sophie had thanked her profusely. (She had been hoping to date Raj.) So yeah, those two "positions" would work. She would give more thought to the résumé during the hour of Chapel that night. Teresa had found that this was an excellent time to think things through, mull over the goings-on at the convent, and devise plans.

So that evening at Chapel, she fantasized about her new job in the Valley. She would sit atop the world of international internet marketing, wear slinky hot black tights and jewel-toned tops—jade, scarlet, shimmering gold! She would meet with other movers and shakers in glass-walled offices overlooking the Stanford campus and make scads of money. Maybe she'd even send a monthly donation to the convent, just to remind Catherine that she was a force to be reckoned with. And of course, she would give nice things to good people like Mary Margaret. Maybe even take over marketing for Mary Margaret! That would make Catherine in-*sane*.

Nailing down a job might take a couple months, but that was okay. There were things she could do here. Show Catherine that she wasn't just a wimpy hanger-on, for starters. And the God thing, she might as well scoop up some of that as long as she was stuck here. How? Gemma! She would become BFFs with Gemma, hang with her, pick her brain about how to get God on her side. She suspected she might need some support from God when she got back to the Valley, with all those drugs everywhere you looked. Besides, she truly did want more God, even though the thought of it made her feel shy. Whatever!

As they left the chapel, Teresa intercepted Gemma. "Sister, do you have a moment to talk?" She was pretty sure that Gemma, with all her Indian stuff and those Himalayan lama pals the other nuns whispered about, didn't go in for the "sister" business. But hey, it was part of the nun game they all played.

Gemma seemed surprised. "Of course, Sister." They walked in silence to Gemma's room. Gemma opened the door and held out her hand for Teresa to go in. Entering that room was like falling down a rabbit hole, Teresa thought. She had never seen so many candles, statues, beads, incense burners, animal gods, or Indian trappings outside of the head shops on Haight Street. Fun to think that all this was tucked away behind a door that looked just like all the other doors. It was as weird as Mary Margaret's room. As Hindu-y as Mary Margaret's was Catholic-y. She wondered what Mary Margaret thought of Gemma. And what Gemma thought of Mary Margaret. Sometimes she just loved the convent, with all its freaky god-women. She would miss that part of it.

"Whoa! You have quite a setup here!" she said. As soon as the words were out, Teresa wished she could take them back. They sounded sacrilegious somehow, but she hadn't known what else to say. Gemma smiled noncommittally. Teresa spotted a small statue of a weird-looking guy with a pointed hat and four arms, dancing in a circle of fire. Her kind of saint, or whatever they had instead of saints. "Who's this?" she asked, moving toward the statue but sensing that she should not touch it.

"Shiva," Gemma said with an indulgent smile. "Won't you sit down?"

"Oh yeah. He's like, what? The God of Destruction, right?" She'd picked up that little shard of esoteric knowledge from Raj Singh when he was showing her around his Ayurvedic cubbyhole at the Ananda Center. Raj hadn't bothered to tell her what Shiva looked like—the funny hat and all that fire, not to mention the four arms—or she could have seemed even better informed.

"Right."

Having reached the limit of her knowledge of things Indian or Hindu, Teresa felt out of her element. In new situations, she had begun to adopt a WWCD (What Would Catherine Do?) tactic. So instead of jumping in with, "See? I know stuff!" she simply nodded and sat as regally as possible on the corner of the bed. Now what? She had learned through painful experience with Catherine that lying, or even dissembling, could lead to disaster. The truth was usually the best path forward. It rarely got you into any more trouble than you were already in, or any more trouble than a lie would, and it was a lot easier to remember.

"Um, I don't know quite how to put this, but it seems like you've got the goods when it comes to God."

"Well, I wouldn't…"

"Yeah, you do." Teresa nodded vigorously. "I don't. I mean, I've read stuff." Her eyes drifted toward Shiva, the site of her recent triumph. "And I've been around here a year so I've heard stuff. But I don't have any, you know, *experience* of it. Him. It." She had hoped that Gemma would jump in at that point and give her the whole God download, reveal all the secrets and initiate her or something so she could take all that power back to the Valley. But Gemma just looked at her with this curious half smile. She forged on. "So, you have this, right? God?" She didn't like sounding so naïve, but didn't know what else to say.

"I practice so I can come closer." What? What did that mean? She didn't have time to learn a whole new language. Okay, back to the truth.

"I want to know about it. How do you get it?" The weird half-smile again. Enigmatic. Teresa wished Catherine had a podcast or youtube channel where she demo-ed how to handle situations like this. Something she could watch to get ahead of the game.

"Well..." Gemma seemed to start down one track, then think better of it and go down another. "Why do you want it?'" Again, back to the truth.

"I may not be here forever—and where I'm going, I'll need God."

Gemma looked concerned. "Are you ill?" Jeez, Gemma thought she was dying! Should she let her think that? Would it speed up the process, prod her along a faster route to the God info? No, that kind of lie could get her into all sorts of trouble, and Catherine would ferret it out for sure.

"Oh no! No! But I may be leaving the convent." She shifted on the bed and didn't respond to Gemma's questioning look. "And I want to get whatever I can before I go. Right?"

"Okay," she said slowly. "How much time do you have?"

"Is this like Confession? Confidential? Just between you and me?" Gemma nodded. "Probably a couple months. I have to get a job first. In the Valley."

"Ah! That sounds exciting!" She gets it, Teresa thought. She gets me. She's impressed.

"I'm not sure how much can happen in two months, but…" Gemma gave her a look and Teresa felt as if her whole soul had been scanned in some sort of spiritual MRI tube. "You'll only get as much as you put in. If you fudge or cheat, you won't get as much."

Teresa nodded eagerly. "Sure! I know!" Did she look like the kind of person who would fudge or cheat? Maybe to Gemma, with her MRI-vision.

"Okay." Gemma rose, went over to a small bookcase, and returned with Thomas Keating's *The Human Condition*. "Read this, and try doing Centering Prayer. It's an easy 20-minute meditation. You can find it online. If you want to talk again, we can."

Teresa snatched the book from her and held it to her chest. "Great! Thank you! This is just what I wanted!" It seemed like Gemma should be more excited about having her as a student, maybe giving her more instruction, practicing this stuff with her or something. But probably the holy nun was testing her, seeing how much she could or would do on her own. That's what Catherine would do. They were all alike! Still, she could put up with it from Gemma, who at least wasn't as self-righteous as Catherine. It was a good return on investment. God, for a little googling.

"It's all about quieting down your mind…" Gemma seemed skeptical, almost as if she didn't think Teresa's mind could be quieted. "I'm not promising anything…"

Teresa held up a hand. "I know. But I can do this." She was ready to leave with her treasure, but Gemma gave no indication that the interview was over. Rather, she leaned back in her chair and gave Teresa a real smile, not the weird enigmatic one.

"What are you going to do down in the Valley?"

"Oh, international internet marketing. That kind of thing."

"Hm. Do you know anything about phones?"

What was it with these nuns and their phones? But wait, maybe she'd get to talk to the Tibetan monks! An intriguing entry for her résumé. Just a cryptic "Consultant to Tibetan lamas in their quest for world peace."

"Some."

Gemma pulled a phone from the pocket of her robe and handed it to Teresa. The cover was a picture of an Indian guy sitting cross-legged, his right hand held up in a kind of "Yo!" greeting. His eyes were hooded and a tiny elephant sat on his right shoulder.

"Shiva," Gemma said with that same cryptic smile, but quickly turned serious. "I'm having a little trouble talking to my friends in Tibet. Can you see what might be wrong?"

Teresa leaned back against the wall and began fiddling with the phone. She was tempted to check out Gemma's browsing history, but didn't want to get caught. Her examination shows nothing amiss. On her own phone, she googled the problem.

"Okay," she said after a few minutes. "I can't see anything wrong with your phone. But I found a story about the Chinese blocking Tibet. That's probably what's wrong." She handed back the phone and Gemma slipped it into her pocket. She looked worried. "Are your friends okay? I mean, could they be in trouble?"

Gemma shrugged. "Hard to know. But thanks for your concern." She was disappointed that Gemma hadn't seized the opportunity to confide in her—but anyway, she'd had enough of India, of Tibet, and frankly of the mysterious Gemma for the moment. For some reason that she couldn't quite figure out, it was exhausting to be around Gemma.

"Thanks!" Teresa said. "Talk soon?"

Gemma nodded, swept a little card from her desk, and slipped it into Teresa's hand as she left. In her own room, Teresa held it under the light to examine it. Shiva! The four-armed fire-dancer. She propped it up against her bedside lamp and began to google everything in the picture, starting with that menacing-looking trident he always seemed to have handy.

*

Gemma was baffled. After six blissful, quiet years in which nobody paid much attention to her or showed the slightest interest in Truth, her room had suddenly become a quick-stop dispensary for enlightenment. First the "prioress" herself, the one who took care of everything and somehow kept the place going. It had been painful to feel her distress, and the deep unhappiness beneath it. She was sure Catherine would be able to work through the distress—that was probably just about surface-level convent issues like finances, at which Catherine seemed quite adept—but the loss of intimacy with the One, that was heartbreaking.

And this new one, Teresa. She was like a mosquito, buzzing around, looking for immediate sustenance. How had she ever landed here at the convent? Still, she was oddly endearing—a word Gemma suspected that Teresa would not like, preferring something like "mighty" or "a force of nature." On her way from the convent to "The Valley." Good heavens.

Gemma lowered herself to a soft green and peacock pillow and sat cross-legged. Gazed into the flame of a flickering crimson votive candle and let herself slip into awareness of the Whole, the reality that we are all One—the candle, the other nuns, herself, the entire universe, all fashioned of the same substance, pulsing together in an infinite field of creative consciousness. She breathed in, breathed out. Let joy flood her, let love flow out to all the world and beyond. Especially to Tibet. For an hour, she sat perfectly still, subsumed in the Divine.

Then she rose, drank a glass of water, and got ready for bed. She lay looking at the ceiling, thinking about her friends in Tibet. Tried to call them again, and again was jammed.

Sleep usually came easily to Gemma, but she didn't generally experience disruptions in her connection to the monks or have two "sisters" knocking on her door demanding immediate deliveries of the Divine.

Something must have scared Catherine when she first got back from India with her new awareness. Something that made her run back to everyday reality and put her connection with Oneness under wraps, rather than nurturing it. Teresa was a much easier case. She had no clue about the One. If she had any idea what it was about, she would run for the hills. What the Girl of the Valley wanted was power, a place to stand in the world, a stronger and better ego. Gemma doubted she could turn that around. Life hadn't yet brought Teresa to her knees. And she had done drugs, lots of them. Gemma could see it in her eyes. Probably speed. She'd given her *The*

Human Condition and Centering Prayer—two classic entry points to spirituality—but had little hope that Teresa would take to either of them.

And it wasn't just Teresa and Catherine. The whole convent seemed to be in spiritual upheaval, and now she herself was being drawn into the web. She recalled the odd interaction she'd had with Sister Julian, a woman with whom she hadn't exchanged a hundred words in the whole three years Julian had been there. They had wound up sitting next to one another at breakfast. As the huge platter of steaming scrambled eggs with cheddar cheese and green onions was passed, Julian had scooped an extra dollop onto her plate.

"Gotta get my protein," she had said, winking at Gemma. Gemma could not recall the last time a human being had winked at her. "Tournament practice this afternoon! Pickleball!"

"Oh?"

"Do you play?"

"What is it?"

"Like tennis, but on a smaller court, with big ping pong paddles and a whiffle ball," Julian had said as if she were explaining the key to everlasting happiness. "It's totally addictive!"

"Ah."

"You should come with me. Did you ever play tennis?"

"Yes. I was pretty good." Where had that come from, bragging about tennis?

"Then you'd *love* pickleball. Come with me tomorrow afternoon. If you like it, maybe you and I could set up a court in the basement. Yeah!" Gemma smiled. "Okay, gotta go. Think about it." And with that, the tall, lanky Julian had swept up her plate, deposited it the kitchen, and loped away.

And so after six years of little, if any, connection with the women at the convent, Gemma had in the course of one day received three urgent requests: two for God and one for a pickleball partner.

She looked at the clock. 10:30. She had been in bed for an hour without sleep. Not surprising, since over the past few days she had felt her attention slowly drifting back toward the world. Wondering about Catherine and Teresa. Replaying the interaction with Julian. Something seemed subtly amiss in the convent. This is how it started, she knew. This is what had happened to Catherine. It was cunning, the pull back into being enmeshed in human interactions and the world's everyday comings and goings. Starting to see those things as your bottom-line reality, rather than as phenomena that had sprung from a deeper Reality that was your true home base. It was no problem when those interests stayed secondary to connection with the Divine, but this was different. This had a whiff of yearning in it, a sideways glance at her old life as a dynamic pharmaceutical sales rep, even her life as a beekeeper and bread-maker. There was some allure in all of that, some excitement after years of quiet contemplation. The truth be told, she was a little bored. That was a red flag. If you were truly focused on Oneness with the Divine, you were unlikely to be bored.

To correct the situation, she got up, wrapped herself in a blanket, and sat for another half hour. By the time she got back into bed, she was firmly seated in the One. She fell into a deep sleep, and dreamed of Catherine and Teresa playing pickleball, Mary Margaret sitting in a high referee's chair, and

Julian shouting encouragement from the sidelines. She herself was selling hot dogs from a small vending cart.

*

The more Teresa learned about Shiva, the less impressed she was. His trident? "A symbol that God was always looking over us," according to Google Images. That sounded like her second-grade teacher, Sister Mary Evangeline. And while the Shiva on Gemma's phone case appeared to have had an elephant sitting on his shoulder, the one on this little card had a snake! Coiled around his neck! "A symbol of fearlessness." Or stupidity. And he was sitting on a tiger skin, which even back then could not have been politically or environmentally correct. The meaning, again from Google Images: "We should not let the wild jungle of this world overpower us. We should vanquish it." What a snore!

She tossed the little card onto her desk and opened her résumé file. The recent additions made it good enough, she figured, and she zipped it out to ten places in the Valley that she thought would be lucky to have her. Then on a whim, she texted her old pal Jessica, who was still at Facebook. "Hey Jess! Just shot out my résumé to some folks, so I'll be back in a couple weeks!" She grinned, feeling as if she were back in the swing of things already. Whoa! Jessica texted back immediately. "Dude, don't send out anything yourself. Work with this headhunter: amanda.shields@gmail.com."

Teresa flushed all over. How mortifying not to have followed the current protocol! Who knew you weren't supposed to approach companies yourself? Immediately, she sent the résumé to Amanda Shields, hoping that the headhunter would jump on it before those ten people to whom she'd just sent it opened her theirs and word of her blunder swept through the

Valley. No reply. What time did Amanda Shields go to bed? It was only 11:00 PM. That had been lunchtime when she'd worked in the Valley.

To pass the time, she flipped through *The Human Condition*, which seemed to be mostly about giving up all the things that made you strong and powerful. Nothing about persuading God to assist you with your projects. Plus, you were supposed to find the Divine within *yourself*. So it was not only dumb, but kind of sacrilegious. The book was a bust. She googled "Centering Prayer," hoping that Gemma's other suggestion would be more productive. The official site, which was done all in pastel colors with a tiny script-like font, probably meant to look like angel wings, laid out the process. It seemed kind of wimpy. You sat comfortably, closed your eyes, and chose a "sacred word" that would indicate that you gave permission to be filled up with "the presence and action of God." Gave permission to God? That didn't seem right.

But Jeez, what should be her sacred word? You didn't want to get the wrong one. Power? Love? Shiva? No! OM was the word! Catherine was always slapping OM symbols up on the convent walls, and Teresa had come across a youtube vid of monks "OM-ing" when she was searching (unsuccessfully) for Gemma's Tibetan pals. So yeah, OM would be her sacred word. You said the word silently, got ready for the influx of God's presence and action, and then if any thoughts came into your mind, you just let them pass through and returned to your sacred word. Hm. But what if it was a good thought, like some great idea for getting a job in the Valley or acing an interview? She supposed she could just remember the thought for later and then go back to the sacred word. That way, she'd be covering all the bases.

She checked her phone. Nothing from Amanda Shields, so she "sat comfortably" in her desk chair. Crossed her legs and folded her arms. Closed her eyes. Opened her eyes and grabbed her phone to make sure it was on vibrate. Closed her eyes again. Said the sacred word. OM! Felt totally ridiculous. Oh wait! That was a thought! Let it go, the instructions said. Where? Oh no! That was another thought! She read the Centering Prayer instructions again. Closed her eyes. OM. Nothing! Where were the presence and action of God? Aaagh. Another thought. After wrestling with the bad instructions and the very flawed Centering Prayer process for ten minutes, Teresa gave up. It simply could not be done. She would let Gemma know that she had recommended a bad, impossible task. Maybe Gemma didn't know that much, after all.

The phone vibrated! Her hands felt clammy as she opened Amanda's email: "Sorry, but I have no fits for this résumé. Suggest you try entry level at ad agencies, LA or Chicago." What? *What?!* This could not be happening. She for shit sure was not going to LA or Chicago, and was not going to work at a traditional ad agency, or at an entry level job. Who the fuck was Amanda Fucking Shields? She texted Jessica, "Amanda didn't come through. Who else?" A long pause, in which Teresa imagined Jessica snickering with their pals Ashley and Jennifer. Finally, Jessica's text arrived. "Dude, if Amanda says no, give it up."

Teresa screamed into her pillow, a "self-expression" technique she had learned at the Ananda Center from primal scream therapist Hughie Langsdorpher. She screamed again, and didn't feel any better. Hughie was full of shit, too! They all were!

CHAPTER SEVEN

SPIRITUAL MISDIRECTION

Catherine dreamed that she was flying through the park to the beach, about three feet above the ground, and the coyote was sprinting along beside her. She awoke feeling almost refreshed, but frowned when she checked her schedule for the day. Three spiritual direction sessions—with Mary Pat, Heather, and Julian. The farther she felt from the Divine, the more uncomfortable she was "accompanying" people on their spiritual paths.

These sessions had devolved over the past year and were now just quarterly formalities, quick check-ins to make sure everyone was doing well and benefitting from their time at the convent—and also opportunities to smooth out any concerns or difficulties. That would be the case with Mary Pat today. There had been some complaints that Mary Pat had semi-adopted a feral cat that lived in the alley behind the convent, feeding the animal in her room and letting it roam freely around the convent at night. Catherine had tried to ignore the reports, hoping that either the objections or the cat would go away, but allergies and fleas had been mentioned, and now apparently the cat even had a name.

Mary Pat was waiting for her in the visitor's chair. Catherine pulled her desk chair around so that they were sitting across from one another, both on the visitors' side of the desk, equal partners before the Divine. It was only then that she noticed the sleek black cat half hidden and sitting, sphynx-like, among the voluminous folds of Mary Pat's robe. Startling emerald eyes stared out at her, and narrowed slightly as she stared back.

"My goodness," Catherine said. "This is a surprise. Is this..." What was the name? Something that rhymed with cat. Bat? Fat? Hat? Mat? Rat?

"Scat!"

"Oh no, she can stay."

"Scat. That's his name!" Mary Pat stroked the cat's back and he began to purr. "And I'm so glad he can stay!" Mary Pat seemed delighted, as if she'd already won some victory. "That mean old Heather is just jealous, isn't she?" Mary Pat crooned to the cat, who rubbed his head against her hand and purred even more loudly. "She just wants a bootiful black kitty all for herself! Poisoning Sister Catherine's mind against us..." The sight of gruff, meatloaf-eating, former-real-nun Mary Pat cooing and talking baby talk to a cat was unnerving. Catherine shifted in her chair. Mary Pat looked across at Catherine and narrowed her eyes just as Scat had done. "Julian likes him! Julian thinks we should buy him a big, cushy pink bed and put it in the kitchen where it's always warm. That way, we can all share him and bring him toys and treats." She paused and returned her attention to Scat, scratching him under the chin. "Jeanne is down with that."

"I see," Catherine said evenly. "Uh, Heather hasn't said anything to me, by the way. But I've had some complaints about fleas and allergies. And some sisters just don't think a cat should have the run of a convent."

"You said he could stay!" Mary Pat boomed.

"I meant that he could stay *here*. *Now*. With *us*. Just for this meeting."

Mary Pat ignored this. "I think maybe he should have a larger role. Become our mascot, of sorts. Come to Chapel, maybe even dinner."

"No. I don't think…"

"But I love him!" Catherine had never witnessed such a deep, heartfelt declaration of love. The depth of that love filled the room and made large, ponderous Mary Pat seem almost luminous. Catherine leaned forward in her chair and gingerly patted the top of Scat's head, then sat back and folded her arms.

"Here's what I'm willing to do. First, take Scat to a vet, get him checked out, and get him a flea treatment. Keep him in your room during the day, with a litter box. You can give him the run of the place at night, but make sure he's back in your room before morning Chapel. On Saturday afternoons, he can hold court in the parlor in that pink bed—but not the kitchen. Have him back to your room before dinner. Okay?"

Mary Pat circled the cat with her arms as she listened, and kept her eyes lowered as she said, "You drive a hard bargain, Sister!"

"I'm a total softie. You got almost everything you wanted." Mary Pat glanced up with a small smile. Catherine added almost as an afterthought, "Is everything else okay for you here? No spiritual crises? Everything okay?"

"Everything is fine. Thank you, Sister."

Catherine shooed her away and managed to return the smile Mary Pat gave her as she closed the door.

What the hell? The allergy people could get pills. The fleas would be gone. Mary Pat and Julian would be happy. And maybe God was love, after all, as people on the Consciousness Circuit always said when they were at a loss to explain the nature of God to their students. In any case, she wished she felt as alive and passionate about anything as Mary Pat felt about Scat.

Moments later, a strange knock on her door. Two hard raps, and a third softer one. Some secret witch's code, no doubt. Heather was always alluding to mysterious, esoteric knowledge that she'd picked up at Moonpath Wymen's Retreat in Sonoma. Always finding deep, occult meanings in a feather found at the beach, a headache, a story in the news.

"Come."

Heather slipped in and draped herself into the chair. Try as she might, Catherine found it difficult not to superimpose over Heather's aubergine robe that long black dress from the forest coven ceremony photo. Sometimes her imagination even added a pointed black hat. She reminded herself to be open and non-judgmental.

"How are you?" she asked pleasantly.

"Are you going to let Mary Pat keep that cat? I saw her in the hall, all brazen and smirky."

"She's keeping the cat in her room, vet-checked and defleaed, with public appearances on Saturday afternoon."

Heather rolled her eyes and shrugged, then leaned forward, elbows on knees, and said with some urgency, "I need to go on retreat. I want to spend a week up near Moonpath."

Heather was usually so laid back and aloof. Urgency seemed out of character. "What's going on?" Catherine asked.

"I feel the Divine River surging within me. Life-giving, full of new energy, new movement. A Rushing River of Rejuvenation!"

"Aha! Say more."

"I've been stagnating. Depressed and purposeless. Then out of nowhere, I felt this new surge of the goddess in me. Maybe it was the new herbs from Chinatown, but I don't think so. I'm brimming with the Divine Feminine, about to burst. I want to contemplate how to direct all this energy and life force. Go back to my spiritual roots, spend some time in silence up in Sonoma, discern where to go from here. I don't really need your permission. I could just go. But I'm asking."

Catherine was tempted to quiz her about just where, and how, she had found this Rushing River of Rejuvenation. How had Heather managed to snag redemption from torpor, when she herself could not?

"Would you stay at Moonpath?"

"Nah, there's a Best Western just up the road. Quiet, sterile, perfect for getting down to the bones. I'll visit Moonpath, but I think that's mostly in the past." She sat up straight, folded her hands in her lap, and fixed Catherine with a sly smile. "You're surprised."

"I am."

Heather laughed. "Life is change, Catherine. I've been given a gift, and I know it. Now I need to find out how to use it."

"Will you come back here when you're clear?"

"Maybe. Probably. I just want to reset, and I need to get away to do that."

Should she just let people come and go as they pleased? What about commitment? What about discipline? But Heather was right. She didn't need permission. And going up to Sonoma to plan a new life was not something that Catherine wanted to forbid.

"Sounds like a plan. When do you want to leave?"

"In a week."

Catherine nodded. "I hope you'll share what you learn—if you come back."

Heather smiled in a very non-witchy way, actually in a very wise, Gemma-like way. "Want to come with?" Catherine was caught off guard, but returned the smile.

"I don't think so. But thank you. And good luck."

Heather reached over and put a hand on her arm, then stood, turned, and glided away.

Catherine sat looking out the window for some time. The quiet mind of spiritual director mode lingered a while, but slowly, insistently, the fretting began again. This little Moonpath alumna had been given, apparently for free, what she herself wanted more than anything. So had Mary Margaret. What was she, spiritual chopped liver? As far as she could tell, neither Heather nor Mary Margaret had done any of the serious meditating that Gemma had recommended for her. What did they have that she didn't? What was she doing wrong, that her path felt completely obstructed while everyone else was just waltzing into nirvana?

*

At mid-day Chapel, Catherine found herself too disheartened by her recent failure even to attempt a union with the Divine. Instead, she resigned herself to spending the hour either staring at the backs of her eyelids or mulling over convent problems, neither of which was particularly elevating. After what seemed like about three days, Sister Jeanne rang her little bell and Chapel was over.

Catherine downed a quick lunch and headed back to the office for her third spiritual direction session of the day. Julian. The pickleballer never had much to say of a spiritual nature, so Catherine decided to fill the void with a longshot question about Julian taking over the prioress job someday—even though that day seemed increasingly remote. But who knew what might rise to the surface with even a random question?

Julian peered around the door jamb of Catherine's office with a quizzical look.

"Come in, Sister. Have a seat."

Julian swooped in as if she were going for a wide forehand and landed in the visitor's chair. Catherine folded her hands on her lap, leaned forward, and smiled warmly.

"How are you, Sister? We don't often get a chance to talk. So busy..."

"I'm great." Julian fidgeted in the chair, as if it were difficult for her to sit still. "Enjoying the sunshine!"

"Ah, yes. Getting outside, are you?"

Julian suddenly seemed wary. "Yes. Outside."

Catherine leaned back and smiled again.

"Sister, have you ever considered taking on more responsibility here?"

"Am I not doing enough? I can do more! Just tell me what to do." She seemed eager to correct anything that might be wrong, and relieved that they were no longer talking about "outside."

"You're doing fine." Catherine paused, wondering why Julian seemed so uneasy. "It's just that at some point, I may be looking to step back a bit, turn over some responsibilities, replace myself eventually. I was wondering if you might consider taking over a few..." Julian appeared horrified, raised her hands to the level of her face and waved away the prospect. "In the future," Catherine said pointedly, realizing even this small opening seemed too much for Julian. "Perhaps the *distant* future."

"Oh no, I could never do that!" Julian's eyes darted from side to side. She looked like a caged animal. "Never!"

"Why not?" Catherine grinned, hoping she might jolly Julian into stepping up or at least find out why the prospect was so upsetting. "You'd be good at it."

"No. I could not do that. Absolutely could not. No." Catherine let the silence fall, again hoping to learn more. "Nope," Julian repeated.

Hopeless, Catherine thought. Okay, she would at least probe for the source of Julian's distress. She didn't need any more surprises. She changed gears and feigned more concern than she actually felt at that moment.

"Is something wrong?"

"No," Julian said flatly.

"Well, Sister, I sense that there is. What is it?"

Julian looked at the floor, out the window, and finally at Catherine. "I have a new passion."

Catherine smiled indulgently. "I know you love pickleball. That's wonderful!"

"I love it more than I love God!" The words came tumbling out. Julian seemed awash in guilt. "All I want to do is play. I'm getting ready for Indian Wells. Big tournament!"

Catherine narrowed her eyes, not really able to discern the problem. "You can play...Indian Wells. There's no rule against that. You can have all the time you need."

"But that's *all* I want to do," Julian said, again looking at the floor. "I think I've lost my commitment to God. I'm sorry. Do you want me to leave?" She sounded almost hopeful.

"No, no. I don't want you to leave. Play as much pickleball as you like. Let's just sit with this. Let it settle."

Julian seemed relieved. She clasped her hands in front of her face and gushed, "Thank you, Sister. Can I go now?"

"Of course," Catherine said softly, and stared after Julian as she strode out of the room.

Catherine leaned back, clasped her hands behind her head, and stared at the ceiling. Completely out of control. All of it. All of them. And they all seemed to have some new passion. Mary Pat's cat, Scat. Heather's River of Rejuvenation. Julian's pickleball. Mary Margaret's Facebook crusade. Maybe that's all the Divine was, passion. Whatever it was, everyone seemed to have it except her.

CHAPTER EIGHT

A WALK IN THE PARK

After the spiritual direction session with Julian, Catherine realized that she had not been outside all day. She pushed herself out of the chair and headed for the kitchen where, as expected, she found Teresa washing dishes with Sister Jeanne drying. Catherine took the dishtowel from Jeanne and waved her away.

"You don't have to do that," Teresa said glumly, glancing at the towel but not at Catherine. So moody, Catherine thought. Where did she get that chip on her shoulder? What did she have to complain about?

"Oh, I enjoy drying dishes! It makes everything feel fresh and clean," she said with a big smile, pleased to be sounding so much more chipper than she felt. Teresa gave her a skeptical sideways glance. "How are you doing?"

"Fine!" So angry she couldn't or wouldn't hide it, Catherine thought.

"Okay," Catherine said evenly. "And how is Sister Mary Margaret?" Teresa focused intently on the coffee mug she was washing.

"I think she's fine. I've been busy, so not as much spying as before." She sounded bitter. Something had changed.

"What's going on? Why are you so busy?" She paused, "And pissed off?"

Teresa handed her the coffee mug to dry. "Do you know anything about Centering Prayer?"

That was the last thing Catherine expected to hear. "Um, a little. It's a way for Westerners to meditate without seeming all Buddhist or Hindu. Why? Did someone at the Ananda Center tell you about it?"

Teresa was silent, and Catherine watched the wheels turn. Could this girl still be considering whether or not to lie?

"Sister Gemma suggested I look into it." The truth! How on Earth had Gemma and Teresa wound up talking about Centering Prayer? "Have you tried it?" Oh brother. The last person with whom Catherine wanted to discuss her spiritual condition was Teresa.

"It's very popular. I'm glad you're doing it," Catherine replied. In her wildest dreams, she could not imagine Teresa sitting still for twenty minutes, deliberately letting go of every thought that popped into her jittery mind and abiding in mental and emotional silence. "Sister Gemma is a wise soul," she added, broadening the conversation in hopes of finding out more about how the two of them had connected.

"Yeah. But Centering Prayer doesn't work for me. It might be a hoax!" Catherine chose not to engage that line of thought, and nodded noncommittally.

"Well, keep at it. It works for a lot of people." That was enough about Centering Prayer. There were bigger fish to fry. She shook out the dishtowel and hung it up. "Let's take a walk."

They crossed Fulton into the park and walked in silence along JFK Drive until they got to the enormous music concourse, which was flanked by the DeYoung Museum, the California Academy of Sciences, and the Japanese Tea Garden. At one end of the vast expanse was a band shell, and in the center, the Rideout Fountain with its huge stone sculpture of a saber-toothed tiger wrestling with a snake. The snake was poised over the tiger and seemed ready to strike. Teresa scowled up at it.

"Snakes," she said, almost to herself.

"Pardon?"

"I've been studying Shiva. He had a snake curled around his neck. What a drama queen!"

Catherine nodded as if she understood. Shiva? That sounded like Gemma, too. Why was their resident mystic serving up a combo plate of Hinduism and Centering Prayer to, of all people, Teresa?

"Let's sit," Catherine said, gesturing to a bench near the fountain. They watched the tumbling water for a moment before Catherine spoke. "So you're doing Centering Prayer, it isn't working, and it might even be a hoax. And you're finding Shiva to be a drama queen. Forgive me, but none of this strikes me as particularly 'you.' I don't doubt that you're upset, but I want to know what's really bothering you."

Teresa pulled back and looked at her with hooded eyes.

"Really? You want to know?"

"Yes."

"Okay, I applied for work in The Valley and didn't get it. Yeah, I was planning on leaving. Still might." This did not surprise Catherine in the least, and she was pleased to find Teresa in truth mode.

"I see. Where would you go?"

"Don't know. Yet."

"That's very interesting, because I've been thinking of leaving myself someday," Catherine said casually. It wasn't a complete lie, and knocking Teresa off her pins a bit might shake loose some information. Teresa looked askance.

"What?! You can't leave."

Catherine gave her a friendly smile. "Of course, I could. If I wanted to. It wouldn't happen tomorrow, or the next day. But maybe someday..."

"You can't leave," Teresa said again. "The place would fall apart!"

"What do you care? You'll be gone."

"I might be gone. But you have to stay."

"No, I don't." And then something occurred to her. Something that might rattle loose even more truth. "Not if I found a replacement."

Teresa leaned away and swiveled toward Catherine. "Like who?" Her expression was half eager, half suspicious.

"Well, I talked to Sister Julian, but she wasn't interested," Catherine stalled. Was Teresa really as interested as she appeared to be? And if so, could she let that happen? No. Teresa was too young, too jumpy, only marginally interested in the Divine—but nothing was certain these days.

"Pickleball," Teresa said dully. Catherine nodded.

"If you weren't leaving, maybe you'd be interested," Catherine ventured.

Catherine gazed at the fountain and, out of the corner of her eye, saw that Teresa's mental wheels had shifted into high gear. A slight frown, but eager eyes. A seagull screeched above them, making quite a fuss, and ultimately landed on the snake's head. A welcome diversion, Catherine thought. Time to exit the potential prioress subject, and let Teresa stew in it for a while.

"See?" Catherine said, gently nudging Teresa with her elbow and directing her attention to the fountain. "The snake is about to be baptized in guano. He's not so fierce after all. Have you ever been to the Japanese Tea Garden?"

They entered through the main pagoda gate and wandered for a while amid the raked sand Zen gardens, koi ponds, stone lanterns, rounded moon bridges, and stepping stone paths. Finally, they found a little table in the corner of the patio café and ordered tea. Catherine was thinking about dangling a little more authority at the convent, but Teresa was staring past her, wide-eyed, at something on the other side of the café. Catherine turned to see what had captured her attention. At a table about twenty feet away sat a young man scribbling into a notebook...and Sister Mary Margaret.

"Oh my God," Teresa whispered. "I lost track of her. I'm so sorry. Who the hell is that guy?"

Catherine pursed her lips and gave Teresa a dour "I told you so" look that did not come close to expressing her actual level of irritation. This was precisely what she'd wanted to avoid. "I'd say he's a reporter," she said dryly.

"I'm really sorry. I don't think she saw us. We can sneak..."

"We'll do nothing of the sort. Follow me."

Catherine rose and started toward the other table, with Teresa in her wake. When she was about halfway there, Mary Margaret glanced up and saw her coming. At first, she looked as if she might bolt. But instead, she shifted to defiance and stared Catherine down as she approached.

"Sister!" Catherine said pleasantly. "How wonderful to find you here on such a beautiful day!"

Mary Margaret froze for a minute, then looked furtively at the young man, and back at Catherine.

"This is John Conlon. From the *Chronicle*. Sister Catherine, our prioress. And Sister Teresa."

Catherine nodded and smiled at the russet-haired young man who couldn't have been more than twenty-five. Conlon stood and held out his hand to the empty chairs at the table.

"Won't you sit down, Sisters," he said. His smile was a little too broad, Catherine thought, and his manner a little too eager.

She smiled at Conlon as she sat. "Thank you, John! What a lovely morning!" She extended a graceful hand, indicating the beauty all around them. "How do you two know one another?"

Conlon glanced at Mary Margaret, but she seemed paralyzed so he jumped in. "My aunt is a big fan of Sister. She told me about Sister's Facebook following, and her message. It sounded interesting." Catherine nodded and glanced over at Mary Margaret, who was facing the sun and looked overheated.

"And what have you discovered?" she asked. "Is it interesting?"

Conlon flipped back through his notes, not looking at Catherine. "Well, a lot of people think she has a very important message, in a new medium, for a new time—and that she's a very special messenger." He grinned conspiratorially at Mary Margaret. "A message we need right now. Let's see…'We are all God. That's all we need to know. If we know that, we will be happy.'"

Catherine smiled noncommittally, then said as if this were hardly news. "That's it?"

"That's enough. It's a powerful message."

"Yes, it is."

"A lot of people will be interested."

"I suppose so."

Catherine turned to Mary Margaret. The old nun was taking short breaths and perspiring. She looked on the verge of fainting. "Sister, I'm concerned that you're getting a little too much sun. Sister Teresa, will you take Sister Mary Margaret home and make sure she rests?"

Teresa cast Catherine a disappointed look. Clearly, she did not want to leave the table. Mary Margaret ignored the prioress's directive and turned to Conlon.

"Now, John," she began, but seemed to lose track of where she was going.

Catherine raised her eyebrows and Teresa was out of her chair, hovering over Mary Margaret. The old nun batted her away, but Teresa put a firm hand under her elbow and murmured, "Come along now, Sister, it's time for your nap. I think we have some brownies left from last night." Teresa narrowed her eyes at Catherine as she gently lifted Mary Margaret to her feet.

"Thank you, John," Mary Margaret cooed. "I enjoyed our talk. And please give this to your aunt." She extracted a small card from her pocket. As she handed it to Conlon, Catherine saw that it was imprinted with her own image and the words, "Love to all. Sister Mary Margaret."

Conlon stood and bowed to Mary Margaret. "Thank you, Sister. I'm sure she'll treasure this. And I'll be in touch!" He tucked the card into his breast pocket. Catherine wondered which of her charges had made the trip to Fed Ex on Mary Margaret's behalf to design and print those cards.

When Teresa and Mary Margaret were out of earshot, Catherine turned to Conlon. She would have bet that he'd been taught by nuns. The Irish name, the familiarity with all the little courtesies. She sat up perfectly straight and looked down her nose at him, hoping to recreate some of the awe and fear in which young boys often held the nuns who taught them. Silence, she knew, would be better than anything she could say. For an instant, he looked ten years old, but quickly returned to reporter mode and leaned back in his chair.

"So what do you think, Sister? Are we all God?"

"Do you hear how that sounds, John? It sounds like you want to write a sensational story at Sister Mary Margaret's expense. I'm sure you're aware that people would mock her if you wrote that."

"Well, do you believe it?"

"My beliefs aren't at issue here."

"Sure, they are. This is what your so-called convent is all about, right?"

"Sister Mary Margaret told you about her own beliefs. Her choice of words may have been misleading. I wouldn't want you to misinterpret what she said."

"What do you mean?"

Catherine fought the instinct to spar with him and instead presented him with an off-ramp, a way to justify not using Mary Margaret's provocative statement. "I'm sure you know the difference between the idea that there's a drop of divinity in all of us and the melodramatic phrase 'We are all God.' Especially when it comes from an older person who seems…eccentric."

"You don't want her going public?"

"I'd prefer that she not open herself up to misinterpretation and possible harm."

"Are you going to shut her down?"

"Of course not. Sister Mary Margaret can do whatever she wants." Catherine smiled serenely and decided that he had enough to chew on for now. "Let me give you my number in case you have any questions." She extracted a small black notebook and scribbled her number, tore out the page and pushed it across the table to Conlon. "I don't have a business card." Their eyes met at this oblique reference to Mary Margaret's personal holy card.

Conlon rose when Catherine did, saluted her with his pencil, and said, "I'll be seeing you, Sister."

"Perhaps."

She turned and walked back toward the convent. She was ready to be away from it all. Away from Julian and her pickleball addiction. Away from Teresa with her total lack of surveillance over Mary Margaret and her burgeoning interest in snakes, Shiva, Centering Prayer, and escaping the convent. Away from Mary Margaret with her selfie holy cards and intermittent dementia. And away from cagey John Conlon.

She went directly to her office and closed the door, determined to finish Chapter 3 of *The Captain's Captive* before dinner.

CHAPTER NINE

THE UNHOLY ALLIANCE

Teresa made Mary Margaret lie down when they got home, and sat in the desk chair to monitor her.

"How are you feeling, Sister?" she asked, trying to focus on the old nun rather than fantasizing about what Catherine was saying to John Conlon back at the Japanese Tea Garden.

"Oh, I'm fine, dear. Don't fuss over me." Mary Margaret let out a little cackle and finally couldn't contain herself. "Don't you wish we were back there, flies on the wall, watching Catherine the Great rake that sweet John Conlon over the coals?"

"You think that's what she's doing?" Teresa asked, hoping she didn't sound too eager.

"Oh, I don't know. Fun to think about, anyway. Isn't it?"

"I guess." Teresa tried to sound neutral. You never knew who might say what to whom. She spotted a stack of Mary Margaret's selfie holy cards on the desk. And next to them, a cardboard box from Vistaprint, the online printing service. She held one up between her second and third finger and asked, "Who got these for you?"

"I got them myself. Online. You can order as many as you want. It's easy. They have wonderful young people who do all the designing."

"And the picture?"

"You just upload it," Mary Margaret said as if she were weary of explaining the obvious. She paused and frowned at Teresa. "I got those cards before they stole my phone. The red phone that *you* gave me. As my own. *My* phone."

Teresa chose not to engage that subject. Instead, she just nodded noncommittally. Mary Margaret turned toward the wall and appeared to go to sleep. A good chance to take stock of where they were. Her first thought was that things could escalate fast, especially with John Conlon in the picture. She might have to make decisions sooner than she'd expected. Catherine had as much as offered her the prioress job—if Catherine ever left. That was a big "if." It had seemed a little out of the blue at first, but when you thought about it, who else was she going to tap? Gemma, with half her mind in the Himalayas? Timid, mousey little Jeanne? Julian in her dayglo pickleball tights? Frowny Mary Pat? Heather, Junior Goddess of the Occult?

The rest were just nice, quiet women whom she hadn't really gotten to know. Maybe she should remedy that. She might need friends if she were going to be the new boss. She could start with the ones she knew a little. It wouldn't take much to win over Mary Pat. Sidle in beside her some Sunday afternoon for a 49ers game and mention some great deal on Omaha Steaks that she'd found online. Maybe get a fuzzy little catnip toy. And Heather... She could ask to buy one of Heather's dreamcatchers, those little spinning, spider-webby talismans made out of string and decorated with colorful beads and ribbons that you hung over your bed. Heather made them late at night down in the basement rec room and apparently sold them at farmers markets and pagan festivals all over the city. At least that was the word around the convent. Yeah, she would show an interest in dreamcatchers. Teresa didn't think either Mary Pat or Heather got much love from the other nuns. It would be good for Catherine to see that those two liked her.

But did she really want the job? It would mean staying here, so she might die of boredom. On the other hand, it might be fun to be in charge and make some changes. Maybe yoga every morning, and she could bring in some of the healers and practitioners from the Ananda Center. For a moment, she allowed herself to think about Parvati massaging little Sister Jeanne's chakras or...

Mary Margaret suddenly sat up straight in bed—she hadn't been asleep after all—and demanded, "What are you thinking about?"

"Nothing," Teresa shot back.

"Yes, you are. You're thinking bad thoughts about me." She paused, then, "Don't lie to me!"

Teresa leaned back and considered the old nun. First of all, she was probably bonkers, so you had to cut her some slack for outbursts like that. Besides, nothing Mary Margaret ever said stung the way that a raised eyebrow or ironic question from Catherine did. Maybe it was because she liked Mary Margaret—at least, she liked watching her cause trouble.

Also, Teresa was beginning to see that Mary Margaret could be an asset. John Conlon was probably going to write something, and he was the freaking *Chronicle!* It was only a matter of time before word of the "sainted old nun over on

Fulton Street" seeped out into other media. A public relations tornado would start to form around the convent and Mary Margaret would be at its center. If she were Mary Margaret's bestie, she herself would be an influencer. It wasn't as if she were using the old nun. Catherine had ordered her to befriend Mary Margaret.

She stood and smiled down at her charge. "Can I get you anything, Sister?"

Mary Margaret glared up at her, folded her arms, and pouted. "No! And don't try being nice to me."

Teresa put her hands on her hips. "How about a cookie from the kitchen?"

Mary Margaret slit her eyes, appeared to mull over this proposition, then smiled beatifically. "That would be lovely, dear. Perhaps a brownie as well, from yesterday?"

Teresa reached down and patted her arm, smiled back over her shoulder as she left. Treats were definitely a way to the old girl's heart. She passed Gemma's door and heard low chanting. She might not even have noticed if she hadn't recently been privy to the odd goings-on in there. She should warn Gemma to get earbuds, or people might get curious about the little ashram she was operating behind her door. She considered stopping in for another God lesson but thought better of it because she'd only tried Centering Prayer the once, when she was waiting to hear back from Amanda Shields, and that had been a disaster. And she'd given up on *The Human Condition* after the first few pages.

But wait! She could sneak in a Centering Prayer session right now. That way, she would feel better about tapping Gemma for another God lesson. She veered off toward the chapel and paused just inside the door to gather herself. Took a deep breath and savored the smell of incense. It always reminded her of being a kid at St. Paul's and going for Visits to the Blessed Sacrament after school. The same amber afternoon light shimmering through the stained-glass windows. The same heavy, holy air. She had really been holy back then. No wonder she'd sought out a convent when she'd broken down.

Anyway, Centering Prayer. She was bound to succeed now, in the quiet and empty chapel. She glided, or imagined she was gliding, to a pew near the front. She sat gracefully, as she had seen Catherine do, and folded her hands in her lap. What was the sacred word? Oh yeah, OM. She tried desperately to quiet her mind. Or at least to focus on "the presence and action of God" in her. But what was God? Who was that? Not the guy she had met at St. Paul's. More like the God, or the Something, that they revered here. How did the convent's *Credo* go? She was able to follow along, kinda, when the others said it aloud every Sunday morning, but couldn't call it up on her own. She grabbed a little card from the missal-holder on the back of the pew in front of her and speed-read:

OUR CREDO

... *hope of grace...love of Truth...living as our authentic Self—the infinite One...creates and sustains all that is...deepen our experience of that Essence...the love, joy, peace, and freedom at its heart.*

Hm. It sounded good enough. Actually, not unlike *The Human Condition*, which she had tossed aside earlier. She would take another look at it, if only to tell Gemma she had read it. Twice! She imagined Gemma could do all those things in the *Credo*. Could Catherine? What about Mary Margaret? Teresa suspected that Mary Margaret's Divinity was closer to the St. Paul's God. She was all about Christ and the Second Coming. But wait, was she? Had Mary Margaret ever actually referred to Christ?

Teresa whipped out her phone and read through Mary Margaret's posts. No! She hadn't. Did she think she was the Christ, the one who was coming to save everybody? An old nun instead of a good-looking Middle Eastern guy? Shit! That would be something. She wouldn't put it past Mary Margaret to see herself as the Savior. Shit again! Could she actually *be* the Savior? She might be a little nutso, but she was onto something and she believed it with all her heart. This was a whole new piece of the puzzle. Centering Prayer would have to wait!

Teresa scurried over to the kitchen. On a gleaming white plate, she arranged six chocolate chip cookies around a central brownie and grabbed two white linen napkins. Then hustled back up to Mary Margaret's room and swooped in with a broad smile. Mary Margaret looked at her suspiciously.

"What took you so long?"

Teresa put the plate down next to Mary Margaret, pulled the chair over to the bed, and selected a cookie. "I stopped to pray." Mary Margaret looked skeptical, but turned her attention to the plate and snatched up the one brownie.

"Really?"

Teresa nodded. "Yes. I prayed for you. For your soul." She began nibbling on the cookie, wishing she had taken a few more minutes to think through her strategy. That's what Catherine would have done. Instead, she had just jumped in and tried to connect with Mary Margaret at the level of God, a terrible idea since God wasn't exactly her specialty, or even familiar turf. She had planted herself on quicksand. Mary Margaret eyed her sharply.

"Why? I'm just fine. You're the one who needs prayers."

Teresa took a breath and rifled at lightning speed through her cache of Catherine tactics. The prime directive, of course, was to tell the truth—especially if the truth was disarming. Mary Margaret loved drama, so a plan that involved both truth and drama would be perfect.

"Sister, I'm guessing you don't have forever to live," she began. Mary Margaret's eyes widened. "Not that you're 'going home' any time soon, but it's always good to be a little ahead of the game, don't you think?" Mary Margaret stared at her, expressionless. "So I'm wondering, where are you going with these posts? What's the end game? Maybe I can help."

Mary Margaret didn't take her eyes off Teresa as she slowly wiped a gooey brownie crumb from her lower lip.

"Do you believe in God?" Mary Margaret asked. Teresa pulled back an inch.

"Of course."

"No, dear. Really. Do you believe in God?" Teresa felt herself blush, something she hadn't done since adolescence.

"I don't know. I want to. I wish I did. I'm trying to." She sounded like an idiot! She must believe in God. She'd sought out Gemma for just that reason. She was trying Centering Prayer, and even about to give *The Human Condition* another shot!

Mary Margaret smiled, reached over and squeezed Teresa's arm. "That's nice."

"I mean, I'm here! Right?" Teresa spread her arms, indicating the whole convent. Mary Margaret smiled smugly.

"Let me see your phone." What? Was the old girl nuts? She'd already had phones confiscated three times! But a flat refusal might set her off again.

"Why?"

"None of your beeswax." Mary Margaret smiled pleasantly and extended her hand for the phone. "Give it. I won't post. What would I post? A picture of you?" Teresa felt vaguely insulted that Mary Margaret's following might not welcome a picture of a younger, up-and-coming convent dweller. But what could it hurt to let the old girl hold her phone for a minute? Anything was better than a big fight with the frail old woman who was moving quickly toward the center of the convent maelstrom. She laid the phone gently on Mary Margaret's palm. The old nun snapped it up and began pecking. Then a pause, and a look of disappointment.

"What is it?"

Mary Margaret just shook her head and smiled. The hand holding Teresa's phone disappeared under the covers. Let it go, Teresa told herself. You just have to get it back before you leave. Better to take advantage of this little break to shift the conversation out of God territory and plant it firmly in the world of public relations. Mary Margaret stared at her, triumphant and self-satisfied. Teresa leaned back in the chair and folded her arms.

"So, tell me what you want. Do you think you're, like, Jesus or something?" She hated hearing the desperation in her voice and forced a detached, Catherine-like tone. "Honestly, I know something about digital public relations. I'd be willing to help, maybe."

"Maybe? Do you want to help me or not? And by the way, what do *you* want?"

"If you're for real," Teresa began, "then maybe your message should be out there. I'm not 100% convinced that you're—pardon me, Sister—*all there*. I mean, I think you believe what you're saying, but…"

"But you think the 'We're all God' statement is too extreme. Sounds crazy?"

Teresa nodded. Mary Margaret rose up off the bed, slipping the phone into her pocket as she moved toward her desk, rummaged around in a rat's nest of papers, and finally found a little *Credo* card just like the one Teresa had held in her hands a half hour earlier in the chapel. She handed the card to Teresa and stood before her. Pulled herself up to her full height, folded her hands at her waist, and recited the *Credo* as if it were the last time she would ever speak.

"We come together in the hope of grace, the love of Truth, and the commitment to living as our authentic Self—the infinite One, the Source that creates and sustains all that is. Our purpose is to deepen our experience of that Essence, and to embrace the love, joy, peace, and freedom at its heart."

She stood looking down at Teresa, who sat frozen with the card in her hand. The words sounded different when Mary Margaret said them than they had in her own mind when she'd speed-read them in the chapel. They sounded true.

"I believe that," Mary Margaret said. "That's what I want people to know. Do you believe it?"

Teresa wanted those words to be true, even if they didn't live in her the way they seemed to live in Mary Margaret. Did that give her the right to say yes? Fake it 'til you make it.

"I do," she said quietly. "And I believe that's what you want people to know."

Mary Margaret sat down on the bed and tilted her head to one side. "But you're right. I may be saying it wrong. Saying it so it sounds crazy. Maybe you could help me with that. With the words."

Teresa gave a little nod, and Mary Margaret nodded back.

"Yeah, the words," Teresa began. "I think there are ways to say it so that…"

Mary Margaret seemed to remember something, extracted the phone from her pocket, and tapped again. This time, a look of triumph. Then the color drained from her face. She shook her head slightly and held the phone out to Teresa with a look of horror.

John Conlon had posted his story to the *Chronicle* site, alongside the ecstatic picture of Mary Margaret.

SF Nun Claims We Are All God

A local nun claims to have a message from above: She is God. And so are you.

"We are all God," says Sister Mary Margaret, 90, who claims that God has been delivering messages to her for the past month. She is passing on her revelations to an avid following via Facebook.

Sister is the spokesperson for an unnamed and heretofore unknown convent on Fulton Street. The Archdiocese of San Francisco denies any association with the "No Name Convent" or Sister Mary Margaret, and released this statement: "We have services to help our older sisters with diminishing capacities, but we have no knowledge of or connection to Sister Mary Margaret or to this alleged convent."

Despite her fans' claims of miracles, both physical and spiritual, not everyone is excited about Sister's message. Among the comments on her posts:

- *This old bat reminds me of my third-grade teacher. F***ing nuts.*
- *These are the words of the devil, designed to ensnare us and cast us into Hell.*
- *Crazy! Go home and go to bed.*

The convent could not be reached for comment.

Holy shit. Teresa slipped the phone safely into her own pocket and began pacing back and forth in the little museum of 1950s Catholicism. She eyed a statue of the Blessed Virgin Mary in her blue mantle, balancing precariously on a little globe, and glared at her. Catherine would shit a brick. This was the nightmare scenario, and Catherine would think it was all her fault for letting Mary Margaret escape. She could come charging through that door at any second, screaming. No, she would be silent and aloof. Punishing. Maybe Catherine would kick her out of the convent. Where would she go? She would have to sneak into the Ananda Center at night and sleep on one of the healers' massage tables!

She looked down at Mary Margaret, who had sunk to the bed and was—Jeez!—possibly crying. Whatever scheme she devised to deal with Catherine would have to include Mary Margaret, and at the moment she did not look very manageable. She met Teresa's gaze and wailed, tears rolling down her cheeks, "This isn't what I wanted to say! God's message is of love. Of hope."

Teresa sat down gingerly beside her and put a tentative arm around her. "It could have been worse..."

"How!?" Mary Margaret said so loudly, so angrily, that Teresa hoped Catherine wasn't lurking out in the corridor, or even on the same floor. Mary Margaret lapsed back into tears and buried her face in her hands.

"There, there. We'll work it out," Teresa said, awkwardly patting Mary Margaret's frail shoulder, trying to sound mature and comforting instead of panicky and out of her depth. How could she keep Catherine from seeing that story? Obviously, she couldn't. Catherine had probably bookmarked the *Chronicle* site on her way back from the Japanese Tea Garden and was checking it regularly.

Teresa wasn't completely surprised that Conlon had written the piece, but actually seeing it in a public forum where hundreds of thousands of other people could read those same words...that put them in a whole new league.

But a plan had already started to take shape in her mind. A plan that would upend everything, and land her on top of the heap.

CHAPTER TEN

SCRAMBLE

Catherine finished Chapter 3 of *The Captain's Captive* with a flourish and snapped her computer shut. She pulled out her phone and perfunctorily tapped in the *Chronicle* site just to make sure that all was still well. She scanned down the headlines and froze. "SF Nun Claims We Are All God…" Adrenalin shot through her. She tapped on the story and read almost without breathing. She couldn't decide whether to unleash her fury on Mary Margaret for the interview, or on Teresa for letting her escape. They might still be together, probably up in Mary Margaret's room. She pounded up the tile stairs, trying to strategize, stifling the urge to scream.

She gave Mary Margaret's door an authoritative knock. Some scrambling on the other side, and Teresa opened the door with a forefinger to her lips. Catherine looked over Teresa's shoulder to Mary Margaret, who lay on the bed with one arm flung across her face.

"Poor Sister is prostrate with grief," Teresa began, wide-eyed. Catherine didn't buy it for a minute and raised her eyebrows. Teresa looked at the floor. "She is so sorry that Mr.

Conlon misconstrued her message." Then in a stage whisper to Catherine, "We need to support her."

Catherine pushed past her and sat on the bed. "I think Sister is just fine." She gently removed Mary Margaret's arm from across her face, revealing a defiant Mary Margaret. "Aren't you?"

"I didn't say those things! I didn't," Mary Margaret said desperately. But then the bravado disappeared and tears welled up. Again, Catherine surmised. Mary Margaret's eyes were already red. She might not be prostrate with grief, but she felt terrible. This situation called for honey, not vinegar. Catherine forced herself into a gentle direction.

"I know, dear. I know you didn't." She patted Mary Margaret's hand. "But that's what he heard, wasn't it? Or what he wanted to hear, so he could write a sensational story."

Mary Margaret nodded slowly. Catherine glanced up at Teresa, who kept clutching and unclutching her hands. The honey was working. Teresa seemed much more malleable than she had a moment earlier.

"What do you think we should do about this?" Catherine asked Teresa, weaving together the little team of three. Teresa drew the desk chair closer to the bed, into the huddle, and sat. She bit her lower lip. Catherine delivered another drop of honey, asking softly, "What is it?" Teresa shifted on the chair and leaned in.

"We need to get control of this. Take charge." Her eyes darted from Catherine to Mary Margaret, and back to Catherine.

"How do you imagine we could do that?" Catherine asked.

"It's bold, what I'm thinking," Teresa said conspiratorially. Catherine kept her face blank. Teresa forged on. "We call the local TV, maybe KPIX. Refer them to the *Chron* piece and invite them here to interview Sister Mary Margaret." She leaned back in her chair looking quite self-satisfied, Catherine thought.

"Feed the fire?" Catherine asked, trying to keep her voice neutral until she figured out whether or not she liked Teresa's plan.

"Get control of the narrative."

"How would that work?" They might be courting disaster with an interview, Catherine thought, but it might just as easily be a good fix.

"We'd have Sister sitting across from the interviewer, with you and Sister Gemma a little behind her." The plan sounded like Teresa had given it some thought. "That way, you could step in if things got out of hand, and Gemma could answer any tricky God questions." Catherine's eyebrow flew up. "I mean, she has spiritual depth, right? That's what we need, right? Maybe she—or you—could do some sort of Jedi…uh, holy…mind tricks on the interviewer. Use The Force on them or something. Only if necessary, of course."

"Where would we do it? In here?" Catherine asked, indicating various features of the little museum: the rosaries tacked on the wall, the statue of Mary balancing on the globe, an ancient and threadbare St. Joseph's missal atop the bookcase, the wall poster of Jesus ascending into Heaven. "Or maybe Gemma's room?" She felt herself drifting toward sarcasm, a bad sign. Stop talking, she told herself.

"We should do it in the chapel," Teresa said quietly but with great certainty, looking pointedly at Mary Margaret, who seemed to have lost interest and was fussing with a frayed thread on her sleeve. "Right, Sister?" Mary Margaret appeared to snap out of it and smiled sweetly at Teresa. "You could deliver your message sitting in the chapel," Teresa said a little too loudly and slowly, as if Mary Margaret were deaf. "We could practice with the words so they would sound sensible and inspiring. Like your message." Mary Margaret nodded vaguely.

Catherine stared at Teresa. The plan was bold, as Teresa had said. And Teresa was right about needing to get control of the narrative, rather than letting it develop randomly and getting overrun by the press, Mary Margaret's fans, smitten Catholics, and curiosity-seekers. But even if the plan made a certain sense, did she dare let Teresa manage it? Could she trust this little techie, turned druggie, turned quasi-nun, turned TV producer? Teresa had skills, but was one of them staging a tableau that looked a little like the Second Coming for the local CBS affiliate in the convent chapel? The plan could work, but it had a lot of moving pieces. Unreliable pieces. A million things could go wrong—and a lot of it depended on the mood in which they found Mary Margaret on the day of the interview.

Teresa had placed her hands on her knees and appeared to be studying them. She seemed lost in what, if it were someone else, might have resembled a meditative state. Very unlike her. Catherine leaned forward and asked quietly, "What is it?"

"There's another piece to this," Teresa said, not meeting Catherine's eyes. Catherine leaned away and steeled herself.

"What?"

Teresa glanced at her tentatively, then launched in. "Well, this could be a kind of gift. You know? We're being pushed into the public arena. Maybe God wants us to do something more public. Like, you know, become a place where people come for retreats and workshops. For spiritual sustenance! A spiritual center!" The idea had jumped into her mind the minute she had started thinking about the interview. It seemed the most natural progression in the world! Even better, it placed her at the center of things. Screw the Valley. She could make her mark here!

Catherine shook her head. "No. Absolutely not! We'll be lucky just to get through the interview. The idea is to keep people way, not invite them in." Somehow, that didn't sound right—but there was no way she was turning the convent into a spiritual supermarket.

"But..."

"Yes on the interview, no on the spiritual center!"

"But..."

"That's it. No."

Catherine glanced at Mary Margaret, who was staring, transfixed, at the poster of Jesus lifting off toward heaven. She turned back to Teresa. "Who will you get to do the interview?" Teresa sighed, apparently resigned for the moment to giving up the spiritual center.

"Rosa Sanchez, I think. She does local features, and it's a good bet she was raised Catholic so she won't fu...mess with us. And I'll prep her to make sure she gets where Sister is coming from."

Catherine nodded and found herself warming to the plan. But she wanted the interview to be carefully scripted. They could...

Mary Margaret flew up into a sitting position and threw her arms into the air. "Hallelujah! There is only one of us here, and we are risen!" Her gaze held to the Ascension poster as she proclaimed this good news, then moved to Teresa. "Do you believe!? Do you believe!?"

"Uh, yes, Sister. Now why don't you…"

"And you. You!" She pointed a bony finger in Catherine's face. "Do you believe we are all one, and risen!?"

Catherine leaned back, folded her arms, and said nothing. She studied Mary Margaret, then glanced over at Teresa and saw that she was about to jump in. She shook her head slightly and Teresa pursed her lips. Catherine took Mary Margaret's hand.

"This is what I believe, Sister. I believe you have a crucial message for humanity at this time. But I also believe you're undercutting that message. Saying it in ways that people can misinterpret, and that can upset them. I know you're enthusiastic, but I want you to start thinking before you speak. I want you to listen to Sister Teresa, and say only the words that she gives you. I know you can do that if you put your mind to it. Focus! Do you hear me?" Mary Margaret stared into space, and Catherine couldn't tell whether or not her words had landed. She spoke a little more loudly. "I want you to use only Teresa's words, so that people can hear God's message. Do you understand?"

Mary Margaret looked at Catherine and narrowed her eyes, but Catherine still couldn't tell exactly where she was. The old nun swerved with incredible speed from inspired to demented, and back again. It was like playing chess with jumping beans. Finally, Mary Margaret nodded, and Catherine realized that was the best she was going to get for the moment. She turned to Teresa and said quietly, "The ball's in your court now, Sister."

Teresa cast her a panicked look, but nodded gamely as Catherine swept out of the room.

On the way back to her own room, Catherine wondered what she had just done. Chosen the best from among several bad options, she told herself. The interview made sense, but this strange, inappropriate spiritual center idea did not. It was all moving too fast, and in ways she could no longer anticipate. She had felt things slipping out of her grasp even before this afternoon; now they seemed entirely out of control. She needed to break the cycle, redirect the energy, stop this downward spiral.

She changed into jeans and a green running top. Stuffed her computer and a few items into her backpack. Then pounded down the stairs and found Sister Jeanne in the kitchen scrubbing pots. She flew past Jeanne and tossed over her shoulder as she headed for the garage, "Please tell Sister Julian she's in charge at dinner, and let Sister Teresa know I'll be back soon."

CHAPTER ELEVEN

RUNAWAY

Catherine gunned the silver Honda north over the Golden Gate Bridge. She felt disembodied, untethered. But that was the point, wasn't it? To untether from all the chaos, the failures and looming threats? To get up above it all and figure out what to do about Mary Margaret, the interview, the convent... and herself?

Then she spotted it, just off the freeway to the right in Mill Valley. The Golden Arches! *That* would certainly redirect the energy. *That* was a place she could be free—and *naughty*. But surely McDonald's was a step too far. She hadn't had a Quarter Pounder, or even eaten meat, in ten years. God knew what was in that burger! But by then she was already halfway down the off ramp, headed toward perdition.

A Double Quarter Pounder, fries, and a chocolate shake. She ate in the car, sitting in the parking lot, huddled over her cache and mesmerized by the nostalgic tastes and sensations. This might be the most delicious meal she had ever eaten, she thought as she emptied another tiny packet of salt onto the fries. The meat was indeed mysterious, but it melted in her mouth, accented by crunchy pickles, tangy ketchup, and succulent little rehydrated onion pieces. The fries were hot to the touch, golden brown and ultra-crispy. The shake was rich, thick, and superbly chocolatey. She felt like an eighteen-year-old runaway-for-a-day, an outlaw satisfying her craving for forbidden experiences. The whole episode was simply delightful.

Back on the road, she headed north toward Jack London Park in Glen Ellen, about an hour and a half north of the city. In the old days before the convent, she had hiked in Jack London whenever her soul felt troubled or uncertain. The redwoods up there held answers, or had in the past.

She turned off the freeway onto CA 37 through the Sonoma countryside, opened the window, and felt the warm wind on her face. Took in the rolling hills, the golden fields and meadows dotted with grazing cattle and dark green stands of live oak. Turned onto smaller side roads lined with stone fences, bright orange marigolds, and fluttering eucalyptus. Ramshackle roadside stands offered glistening half-gallon bottles of dark red cherry juice and local produce laid out on weathered boards. Muted red, ochre, and dusty green vineyards spread out in all directions—and everywhere, earthy scents mingled with the sharper essence of eucalyptus. She pulled over and stood for a moment beside the car, looking out to a vineyard, letting the warm breeze envelop her and slow her down. Popped out her phone, scored an Airbnb room in Glen Ellen for the night, and was there in thirty minutes. The cozy-looking stone house sat on a hill on the outskirts of town, nearly hidden behind trellises of overgrown ivy. A woman with long salt and pepper hair, dangly earrings, and a maroon Indian top that might have been left over from the Summer of Love came through the front door toward her.

"Sally Abilene," she said, offering her hand.

"Catherine Walsh."

"Come on back. I'll show you around."

Sally led her to a private entrance in the back with a tiny patio and two dark green Adirondack chairs. The room was small, hardly big enough for a double bed, closet, little desk, chair, and tiny bathroom. Catherine smiled, thinking how similar it was to the convent rooms, except that the walls were lined in pine, a multicolored hook rug covered the only empty floor space, and the bed held a puffy sage comforter and several small gold throw pillows.

"You have a little coffeemaker under the sink," Sally said, looking around the room as if trying to remember what else to tell Catherine. "Anything you need?"

Catherine shook her head. "I'm good. I'll be taking off early tomorrow."

Sally nodded. "Well, hope you enjoy your stay." And with that, she was gone.

Catherine took a bottle of water out to the patio and watched the sun set behind Sonoma Mountain. Above the green-black oaks and redwoods, the sky broke into tangerine, dark orange, violet, and amber with streaks of brilliant gold. For the first time in months, maybe years, her mind went utterly silent.

In the morning, she brewed some coffee and again sat out on the patio. Should she be thinking more? Taking notes? Journaling? Making lists of pros and cons? Diagrams? Her only thoughts were of breakfast. At the Creekside Café, she wolfed down Crispy Sourdough French Toast and a Spinach and Mushroom Scramble. With real orange juice. It was heaven.

Her phone buzzed. A text from Teresa. She didn't open it.

Jack London Park was ten minutes up a winding road past wineries, fenced-in homesteads, more stands of eucalyptus, and acres of soft undulating grasses. The park itself covered nearly 1600 acres of meadows, mountains, and lakes. Jack had operated a ranch there and it was later incorporated into the state park system. Catherine swung into the Lake Lot and headed up the redwood trail to the lake. It would be a steep climb, but this was the path where clarity had always found her. Red-tail hawks and turkey buzzards circled overhead. Wispy white clouds raced across the bright blue sky. Soon the trail began winding upward into a darker, loamier place on the mountain where the sunlight was dappled and ferns spread out across the reddish earth. Tiny rivulets of water tumbled down over tree roots and red-grey-black fieldstones. A blanket of soft fallen redwood needles hushed the scurrying sounds of small animals.

On either side of the trail, dense towering redwoods nearly blocked out the sun. They seemed to create a force field that enveloped her and made her part of them. Many of these giants were centuries old and knew the wisdom of the Earth, she thought. Each tree had its own energy, but they all sprung from the same root system and that system covered miles. Many grew in fairy circles of trees that had sprouted up out of the roots of a mother tree who had died.

Ten minutes up the trail, Catherine came to a fairy circle where she had sat thirty-five years earlier, newly arrived in the West and wondering if she should stay or move back to Chicago. Over the years, she had sat in that same circle many times, hoping for answers or peace of mind—and for the most part, she had found them. Should she date this one? Take that job? She was already having trouble with the Divine back then, but the finite issues of work and romance had seemed more pressing. She'd figured she had plenty of time to deal with the Divine, and hoped it would just work itself out. Now, she realized that she did not have decades yawning out before her. The Divine had moved to the front of the line and, somehow, it was all tied up with what was happening at the convent.

She stepped off the trail, lowered herself into the center of the fairy circle, and sat cross-legged, not caring that the damp earth and needles ground into her jeans. The redwoods nestled around her. She waited for the epiphany that usually found her there, the clarity about who she was and what to do. But none came. She sat very still for another fifteen minutes, as the mist permeated her running shirt and jeans. Still nothing. Finally, she pulled herself up, brushed herself off, and stepped back onto the trail. Maybe her luck had run out. Maybe she no longer deserved answers. But just then, a whiff of guidance floated through the damp air. Not like the strong directives she'd received in the past, just a subtle reminder. The message: She could find her own way now. That was definitely not what she had expected or hoped to hear. But it was better than nothing, she decided as she headed up the trail.

Farther up the mountain, the redwoods gave way to chaparral that crunched under her shoes. Bright sunlight turned the day hot, and dried her shirt and jeans. So, she was on her own to figure this out. She could always leave the convent and go back to India. Maybe stay there the rest of her life, join up with some ashram or even Mother Teresa's gang. No, she was too old for that. She could go up to Oregon and get a simple job. Maybe be a river guide. How hard could that be? She was an excellent swimmer and kayaker. Maybe Gemma could refer her to the bee-keeping, bread-making place. But she knew that would last about a week.

She was panting and sweating by the time she got up to the lake, and stood with her hands on her hips to survey the area. The lake was coated with reddish algae. A stand of trees on the other side rustled in the wind. A small stone bridge led up to a trail she'd never explored.

Whatever she decided to do, it had to put her back in control. That was the main thing. She'd had enough of letting events evolve on their own, or take shape under the prodding of Mary Margaret or Teresa. She imagined herself on her deathbed—a trick she often used when making decisions—looking back at herself now. What should that person standing by the lake do? What would put her back in charge, and guarantee a good outcome?

Suddenly, it was all clear. The result she wanted was to live inside a deep, intimate connection with the Divine. The two times she had achieved that connection as an adult—in India, and again when they first began intense contemplation at the convent—it had been because she'd worked hard at it. She had ignored all distractions and focused only on that end, to the exclusion of almost everything else. Gemma had been right! And she had reacted to the wise advice like a surly teenager. Sure, she had failed at her first serious attempts—but that was no excuse to give up! She would simply have to work harder.

In fact, it seemed clear that the whole convent should work harder and focus more strenuously on the Divine. Things had gotten too loose. People were coming and going. All the pickleball and dreamcatcher-making and feral cat adoptions were distracting. They were losing their way, slipping into mediocrity, so far from their original purpose that Teresa had actually proposed turning the place into a Consciousness Circuit stopover.

She would go back and set up a serious regimen. Lots of meditation and contemplative reading. Lots and lots of silence. Retreats and deeper spiritual direction. They would read their *Credo* aloud every morning at Chapel and form discussion groups. This would be their new path. Anyone who didn't want to go deeper didn't have to stay. The new program would not be easy, but look what easy had gotten her!

On the way back down the redwood trail to the Lake Lot, Catherine congratulated herself. This trip had been a brilliant idea. She'd just needed to get away to get some perspective and see the light. It felt wonderful to have a plan, a way forward that she could trust and a direction in which to unleash her energy. A purpose and commitment. Even a mission, as Mary Margaret might say. If a mission hadn't been dropped into her lap, as it had been for the others, she had damn well created one!

She looked up to the bright blue sky and the puffy white clouds scudding across it. This answer was almost mathematically guaranteed to solve the problem. All she had to do now was implement it.

The car was hot from sitting in the sun. She rolled down the windows and drove twenty minutes to the little town of Sonoma, where she popped into her favorite bakery and emerged with an enormous, chunky, gooey apple fritter. She texted Teresa that she'd be home that night, and headed back toward the freeway through the lazy golden Sonoma hills. With her eyes still on the road, she reached over to the passenger seat, opened the waxy little bakery bag, and felt around for the crunchiest spot of the fritter—then lifted the pastry to her lips. Deep fried batter, warm cinnamon-y apple bits, and white sugar glaze exploded on her tongue.

All would be well. Surely it would, now that she was back in charge.

CHAPTER TWELVE

HOME ALONE

"Okay, Sister, from the top." Teresa was surprised how quickly Mary Margaret had learned the new words for her message, and how willing she seemed to use them. Conlon's piece in the *Chronicle* had scared her.

Mary Margaret sat up straight in the little desk chair, her hands folded in her lap, and smiled serenely, confidently at her audience sitting on the bed. Teresa leaned forward, the script in her hand, and smiled encouragement. Mary Margaret took a breath and began.

"Thank you for having me, Rosa. My message is really so simple. Perhaps that's why people get confused and make it sound sensational. We all just want to know and love our God, whether we call that god Universal Mind, or Source, or even (amused smile and nod) The Force. Why is that? I think it's because there is a bit of God in all of us. A divine spark, if you will. And I believe we are meant to find that spark and nurture it. That's why I've reached out to people."

Teresa nodded enthusiastically and posed the next question she knew Rosa Sanchez would ask. "Now Sister, it's been reported that you talk to God. Is that true?"

"(humble smile) Rosa, I believe we all talk with God in our own ways. Through intuition, through the love of our family and friends, through those little messages that come to us throughout the day. They prompt us and help us. My intuition has been to spread the word about that divine spark."

"Good! Good!" Teresa said, relinquishing the role of Rosa Sanchez. "You've got it, Sister. You know the other questions cold, and if she asks anything you're not sure of, just repeat those two answers. You're going to be great!"

Teresa truly did believe that Mary Margaret would be great—if they caught her at the right moment. But there was no telling where Mary Margaret's mind might wander, or when. Even now, she seemed to be lost again, staring at the poster of the Ascension.

And Catherine! She had been gone since yesterday afternoon, almost twenty-four hours, and no word. She wasn't answering texts. How could she be so irresponsible? Teresa had already fielded calls from one blogger and two other papers since Conlon's piece had landed. Everybody wanted to get at them, just as Catherine had predicted. But now that they were facing the onslaught, Catherine had disappeared. Teresa couldn't put these media folks off forever, and she desperately wanted the TV interview to be the public's first look at them.

In fact, Teresa's thinking had gone well beyond the interview. She had even imagined a "60 Minutes" segment for Mary Margaret. And far from giving up the idea of the spiritual center, as Catherine had ordered her to do, it now seemed even more obvious that they should launch it during the interview! Catherine would come around. How could she not? Becoming a hub for workshops, classes, and retreats would not only make them a force for good in the world, but solve all their financial problems. In her mind, the interview and launching the spiritual center had already merged into one entity. The confluence seemed almost divinely ordained. "Part of God's plan," as Mary Margaret might say. It almost seemed like a sin *not* to hitch the spiritual center to Mary Margaret's star.

The benefits to the world and the convent aside, the spiritual center would give her a personal mission that was far more altruistic, and certainly sounded better, than going back to the Valley. Fuck Amanda Shields! And Jessica! All of them! She was better off here.

Teresa turned to Mary Margaret. "Sister, you've done so well. Why don't you take a nice nap?"

"Fine, dear. I'm a little tired." She looked very tired, Teresa thought. Saggy and ashen. Maybe it would be better just to let her rest than to practice any more.

On the way back to her own room, it occurred to Teresa—not for the first time—that Catherine might be halfway to India by now and never come back. What would happen to the convent then? She had a plan for that, too.

She was tempted to call KPIX and set up the interview without knowing when, or if, Catherine would return. Of course, it would be ideal if Catherine were there with them in the chapel. Catherine was better equipped than she was to handle weird, out of control situations. What if Rosa brought some random priest, and he started accusing Mary Margaret of blasphemy, and Mary Margaret went berserk and asked him how many altar boys he'd abused that week? Teresa could easily imagine Catherine stepping in with her calm, authoritative presence and making the priest look like a bully who was attacking an old lady, then laying a hand on Mary

Margaret's shoulder and in some magical way making her calm down and seem sane again. But Catherine had totally left her hanging. She would never do that if she were in charge.

Her phone buzzed. A text from Catherine. "Back tonight. Thanks." OMG. Teresa was awash in relief, with just a trace of disappointment. But no apology from the prioress! Who did she think she was?

Back in her room, Teresa called Rosa Sanchez at KPIX—the best choice, in her opinion, because she was a colorful personality and also Latina, so probably at least formerly Catholic and therefore unlikely to give a nun too much trouble. It turned out that Rosa had already read the *Chron* piece and been intrigued.

"So you have a saint over there on Fulton?" Rosa asked in her gravelly voice. Teresa couldn't tell whether the reporter was challenging her or just bantering.

"Come meet her," she replied in a voice that she hoped had a smile in it.

"This is an exclusive, right?"

"Uh, sure." Teresa wasn't exactly certain what she was promising, but Rosa's question was proof that Mary Margaret was fast becoming a person of interest among media folks. She grabbed her public relations hat and parried Rosa's questions about the convent and nuns, describing them as "a community of women meditating for the world's well-being." She shifted questions about Mary Margaret's age into a discussion of "elder wisdom," and rephrased talk of "visions" to "insights into the human condition." She made sure Rosa understood that Mary Margaret was eccentric, but sincere, and genuinely wanted to help people be happier. Not somebody you should push around, or you'd look vicious and abusive.

"How about tomorrow at 2:00?" Rosa sounded so much older than she looked on TV, Teresa thought.

"Perfect," Teresa replied in a gracious, Catherine-like tone. "We can do it in the chapel."

"Can we video chat now so you can show me the layout?"

"Uh, sure. Give me a minute to get down there and I'll call you back."

Teresa suspected that video chatting in the chapel was against at least one rule, or would have been if the rules had anticipated current technology. But a few minutes later, standing at the chapel's center between the altar and the pews, she thought again that it really was a little jewel box. The perfect setting. Who wouldn't like and admire people who worshipped here? She dialed Rosa but turned the phone away from herself and toward the table in front with the large ivory candles and colorful flower arrangement, suddenly shy about letting the reporter see her. Would Rosa be able to tell how far she was from being a real nun, or that she was spearheading a scheme that was in direct opposition to her superior's orders? She swung the phone around to give Rosa a 360-degrees view of the chapel.

"That's gorgeous!" Sanchez said. "Terrific ambiance. Could you speak so I can get a sense of the sound?"

Having given herself that little reprieve, Teresa figured she would have to meet Rosa at some point and better now than right before the interview. She turned the phone toward herself and said with a flourish, "Welcome to our chapel, Rosa Sanchez!" They both laughed.

"Hey, I know you from somewhere!" Sanchez said. "Wait. Wait. Do you hang out at Ananda?"

"Uh, I do some freelance bookkeeping and IT there, yeah."

"I go there! I do yoga three times a week. With Sanjay! Yeah, I thought I recognized you. Okay, tomorrow at 2:00!"

"Right. I'll text you the details."

Teresa closed the app and felt undone. She sank into a pew and knelt—before what, she was not sure. Suddenly, it was all very real. Maybe she just should have stepped away and let the convent twist in the wind. Let the marauding hordes come. No! The other nuns would never have taken control. They'd have been overrun, and with no way to turn that energy to the good. With her plan, they'd be better off than they'd been before! And so would she.

*

Buoyed up by her vision, she texted Catherine the time of the interview—but got no answer. Infuriating! She was sick of having all the responsibility and none of the authority. That would have to change. The universe had given the convent a clear path to success, and she wasn't about to let Catherine wreck it. But to navigate the road ahead, she would need allies. She would have to accelerate her plan to make friends with some of the more influential sisters.

She thought for a moment, then texted Mary Pat, Heather, Jeanne, and Julian and asked them to meet her in the parlor. It was a plain little area just off the dining room, rarely used, with a faded brown sofa that someone must have scavenged from somewhere and a few random arm chairs. Teresa pulled three chairs together for herself, Mary Pat, and Heather. She wanted those two to feel special, superior, as if they were also leaders in the enterprise she was about to propose. Julian and Jeanne could sit on the sofa.

A low-pitched snarl, and Teresa whirled around to see Mary Pat standing in the doorway with Scat in her arms. His bright green eyes flared at her. A small ridge of black fur rose up on his back.

"Scat! Be a good kitty," Mary Pat crooned. The cat snuggled deeper into her arms and rubbed his cheek against her elbow. Clearly, Scat was the path to Mary Pat's heart. Teresa did not like cats, but she'd once had a roommate who owned one and had learned the rules. She took a breath, plumped up her courage, and approached the cat slowly with her hand extended in friendship, stopping when the hand was about four inches from his face. Scat gave her a piercing look, then glanced down at the hand as if he might shred three or four of the fingers, then looked up at her again. Finally, he reached his neck out toward her until his nose touched her fingers. He sniffed once, then rubbed his head against the back of her hand.

"He likes you!" Mary Pat bellowed through a big grin. "He wants to be your friend!"

"Oh. Good. I want to be his friend," Teresa said, forcing a smile. "Why don't you two sit over here?" She motioned toward the most comfortable looking chair and Mary Pat seemed pleased to be given the seat of honor.

Julian strode in wearing orange tights and a white tee, fresh from pickleball apparently. "Hey, I used to practice against this wall." She examined the white wall and rubbed out a few dings with her finger.

"Thanks for coming, Sister. Have a seat on the sofa, won't you?"

Heather and Jeanne arrived at the same time and glanced warily at one another. Heather wore a black dress and a large round bronze pendant. Some sort of ritual item, Teresa supposed. Jeanne's damp hair and white apron suggested that she had come directly from the kitchen.

"Welcome!" Teresa said to Heather, trying to sound occult or at least sonorous. "Please sit here." She held the back of a dark red comfortable-looking chair. Jeanne slipped onto the sofa next to Julian. They greeted one another with nods and stiff smiles.

Teresa sat in the wing chair between Mary Pat and Heather, and held out her hands. "Thank you all for coming. I know you're very busy, so I'll be brief. And I know this may seem a little mysterious, but you are the leaders of our community and I wanted to give you a heads up about some exciting news!" She assumed a gracious Catherine-like smile and told them about Mary Margaret's interview with KPIX the next day.

"Here?!" Mary Pat asked, looking askance. "In the *convent?*" Heather narrowed her eyes at Mary Pat. They were so oil-and-water-y, Teresa thought. She would need to incentivize them to work together.

"This is really more of a community that a cloister, don't you think?" Teresa said pleasantly to Mary Pat. "You're one of the few among us who has lived in an actual convent. I'm not sure many of us would have the strength to do that, or the flexibility to adapt to our way of life as you have." Mary Pat sat up straighter, then leaned back and smiled.

"So the TV people will be *here?*" Julian asked, leaning forward with her elbows on her knees. "Do we have to wear our robes?"

"That would be nice," Teresa said, imagining Julian showing up in her puce dayglo tights. "We don't really have to do anything. Sister Catherine and Sister Gemma will be with Sister Mary Margaret, supporting her. We just need their way." Her mind filled with images of Hea up in one of her cobweb outfits and Mary Pat Chicago Bears baseball cap. "Even out of sight, added.

Mary Pat stroked Scat's cheek. Julian shifted uncomfortably on the sofa. Heather closed her eyes and took a deep, diaphragmatic breath. Their lack of response was a bit unnerving, but maybe they just needed to let the news sink in. Teresa was determined to push forward and lay out the whole plan. If not now, when?

"And that's not all!" she said brightly. "We're thinking of opening up our community, becoming more of a spiritual center. A place where we could share some of the things we've learned with others. It might come up at Sister Mary Margaret's interview, so I wanted you all to know about it first." Blank faces all around. They needed more information. She looked at Heather. "We might present a course on rituals, and how they guide us through life's passages. Or tarot, the I Ching, even channeling." Heather opened her eyes, looked at Teresa, and cocked her head to one side. Better, Teresa thought. They just needed some specifics, and some time. She shouldn't expect them to be jumping up and down—yet. Teresa turned to Mary Pat. "Or deepening our connection with our animal friends as a way to come closer to God." Mary Pat let a small smile play around her lips as she stroked Scat's back. To Julian, "Or the spirituality of sports, like the book *Golf and the Kingdom*."

"Wow," Julian said, rocking back and forth on the sofa. "I can so see that!"

Teresa turned to Jeanne, "Or the ways we serve others through cooking and caring for them." A small, shy smile. More than Teresa had expected from her. This had been a brilliant idea, after all. She had started the process with each of them, and nobody was a cold "no." Heather was the first to speak.

"Does Catherine know about this?"

"We've discussed it. We're still in the 'thinking about it' stage. No final decisions yet. I just wanted to let you four know about it because I think each of you has something unique and important to contribute. I wanted to plant some seeds. Just plant some seeds, that's all."

"I could never teach anyone," Jeanne said, practically in a whisper.

"Oh, you never know, Sister," Teresa said softly. "You might be quite good at it. I know you have a lot to teach *me*." Jeanne's slight nod appeared to be involuntary. Teresa bristled, remembering the many times that Jeanne had stopped the soup from boiling over or pinpointed a missing ingredient when they cooked together. She forged on, expanding the vision. "This would be a chance for all of us to stretch a little. Broaden our horizons. Step through the discomfort as we serve others and the Divine."

Mary Pat frowned slightly. "I'm not sure about this—but if we did it, I think the SPCA could help. Outreach and all that."

Teresa nodded. "That's just the kind of visioning I'd hoped we could do."

"I might not have time," Julian said, squirming on the sofa. "Nationals and all…"

"That's fine," Teresa said. "We don't have to decide anything today. I just wanted you to start thinking about it. And I'm very grateful that you all came and listened."

"Okay, gotta go." Mary Pat said, pulling herself and Scat up out of the chair. The rest stood and headed toward the door.

"Uh, thanks for letting us know," Julian said on her way out.

"Interesting," Heather whispered to Teresa as she passed. A pause, then, "You're good at this." Teresa smiled vaguely, not completely understanding what Heather meant. "PR and all."

"Ah," Teresa smiled back. "Thank you."

When they had all gone, Teresa fell back into her chair. Should she have done that? Was it sabotage? Mutiny? No, just information-sharing. Community-building. Not actually undermining Catherine. Just letting people know what was going on. If Catherine didn't want her doing that sort of thing, she should stay home and take care of business!

As she headed upstairs to get Mary Margaret for dinner, Teresa tried to waft through the corridors the way Catherine always did. Serenely. But let's face it, she told herself, with a little more *Life Force*!

*

Catherine let the warm wind whip through her hair as she sped south through the rolling fields of Sonoma County. A text pinged but she let it go, savoring her last moments of freedom as she merged onto the Golden Gate Bridge. At a stop light a few blocks from the convent, she read Teresa's message that she had already scheduled the interview with Rosa Sanchez. For tomorrow! How had Teresa mustered the nerve to do that without checking with her first? Still, if they were going to do it, they might as well get it done. The sooner they finished with John Conlon and Mary Margaret and the Second Coming, the sooner she could start getting the convent, and herself, back on track. Thank God that all the ambivalence and hesitancy were behind her.

She pulled into the convent garage and entered the deserted kitchen. Where was everybody? She bounded up the stairs, dropped her backpack on her bed, changed quickly into her robe, which projected more authority than jeans, and knocked on Teresa's door. It opened quickly, almost as if Teresa had been standing there waiting for her. She might as well have had a hand on her hip and been tapping her foot, Catherine thought. She didn't invite Catherine in immediately, but just stood in the doorway emanating an unsteady combination of exasperation, anxiety, and flat out pissed-offedness, which she attempted to disguise with a veneer of "Catherine-like haughtiness." It left her vulnerable, Catherine thought.

She stepped past Teresa into the room and sat in the desk chair. Teresa sank to the bed.

"You've been busy!" Catherine began.

"I had to go ahead and set it up! We were getting hounded. I took calls from a blogger, a radio station… If we didn't get control of the narrative… Besides, you said the ball was in my court now." Catherine let the silence extend. "Rosa Sanchez is really nice."

"Do you know her?"

"I showed her the chapel on video chat. And, uh, we texted again this afternoon."

"What did she think of Mary Margaret?"

Teresa pulled her feet up under her and sat cross-legged on the bed, leaning back against the wall. "I told her Mary Margaret was a little eccentric, but authentic and enthusiastic. She'll go easy on her."

"What makes you say that?"

Teresa shrugged and slumped against the wall. "Just a sense. An intuition. She's a good person."

Catherine nodded in the silence, then, "You've talked to Gemma?"

Teresa looked relieved to be talking about Gemma instead of Rosa Sanchez. "Yes! She's on board."

Catherine nodded. "How's Sister Mary Margaret?"

"Good! Maybe a little tired. We've been rehearsing, but I thought I'd let her get to bed early tonight."

Again, Catherine nodded. "Well, it sounds like you have everything in hand." She stood to leave, and Teresa stood with her.

"Wait!" Teresa said, her eyes wide. "Um. There's something else." Catherine raised her eyebrows. "Uh, I know you didn't exactly warm to the idea of us doing workshops and classes here when I first brought it up. You know, making us a spiritual center and all." Catherine narrowed her eyes. "But just listen for a minute. It'll be good for us. Good for PR, good for money, good for the women here. Good for the world! And if we're going to do it, the interview is a perfect time to launch it. While we have people's attention. Kind of riding the coattails of Mary Margaret's mission..." Catherine stared at Teresa in a way that usually shut people up, but Teresa kept going, speaking more quickly and with a note of desperation slipping into her voice. "It seems like a God-given opportunity. Gemma could teach meditation. You could talk about your India stuff. Heather could bring in, uh, esoteric knowledge. Mary Pat, the real Church." And then suddenly, Teresa seemed to lose steam. "Or cats. Or something..."

Catherine tilted her head to one side. Exactly her worst nightmare. The place overrun with seekers lounging in the hallways, glued to their phones and snapping bubble gum.

"Hm. I'm not sure any of that would work. Let's think about it."

"I already told Rosa we were going to do it. I just kept thinking about it, and I knew it was the right thing to do. I told her we'd launch it at the interview."

Catherine was stunned. "I see," she temporized, then let a long silence do its work on Teresa, who was now clutching her fingers. This didn't seem like the time to lay out her own plan. Better to topple Teresa's idea first, then operate into a clear space. But bottom line, she couldn't actually nix the spiritual center idea without seeming like a tyrant—something that would inevitably backfire—or even forbid Teresa to say anything about it at the interview. Teresa didn't have to obey her any more than Heather needed her permission to do her retreat up near Moonpath. Besides, Rosa Sanchez already knew about it and would likely bring it up even if Teresa didn't. She would have to find another way. She took a breath and leaned into the prioress aura of authority. It was all she had left at the moment.

"Have you thought that through?" she asked. Teresa shifted from one foot to the other, but said nothing. Catherine stood up straight and looked down at Teresa. "I wouldn't say anything about it if I were you." She let another second go by, then, "Good night, Sister." She flashed a fake smile and slid into the corridor.

Back in her own room, it felt like everything had turned upside down in the half hour since she'd returned from Sonoma. She had arrived home clear, certain of where she wanted to lead the convent. Now there was a huge barrier in her way. If she were dealing with the old Teresa, she might have simply swatted her away. Deflated her and her plan with a few well-chosen words. But this new Teresa seemed bigger, stronger, and a lot more determined. Catherine had made her disapproval of the spiritual center very clear, twice, and Teresa hadn't even slowed down. In fact, she seemed even more driven. Why? Maybe it gave her an identity, Catherine thought, a reason to be. It made her someone, if only to herself. If that were true, Teresa would cling to it for dear life.

As she got ready for bed that night, Catherine assessed the situation. She had imagined implementing her changes gradually, over time and as softly as she could manage. She had not anticipated a fight, or the need to move quickly. Should she even engage that fight? If she did, she had better win or she'd wind up humiliated and probably having to leave the convent—unless she wanted to become a barker for Teresa's enlightenment baubles. That simply could not happen.

She did not sleep well.

CHAPTER THIRTEEN

READY FOR MY CLOSE-UP

Catherine stood in the back of the chapel, imagining that she was seeing it through Rosa Sanchez's eyes. The place exuded peace, calm, and holiness. The lush plum carpet, the gleaming walnut table up front with the six ivory candles flickering gently. She had lit them herself, just minutes earlier, and Sister Jeanne had added some lavish pink hydrangeas to the bouquet at the center of the table. The afternoon light drifted in through stained glass—green, indigo, gold, peach, and deep red. Perfect. She wished everything could stay exactly as it was in that moment.

She would simply have to ride out the next hour or so. The interview was now inextricably linked in Teresa's mind with launching the spiritual center. She could only hope that Teresa would come to her senses and not mention it, which was unlikely, or else that she would announce it and then meet with strong resistance from the rest of the sisters. Catherine tamped down the wave of *schadenfreude* that washed over her when she imagined all the others rejecting, even scoffing at, the idea of a spiritual center. She was fairly sure that they were no more interested in a spiritual carnival than she was. Teresa's plan would simply dissolve on its own. When that happened, she could step forward with her own new program.

A ruckus in the hallway—several people talking at once, the banging of metal and plastic, Teresa's high-pitched laughter—and the whole group shoved into her holy space. A burly guy with three grey plastic cases hanging from his shoulders. A short, muscular young woman with a flattop haircut, a ring through her nose and tattoos all up and down her hefty arms, carrying a huge camera on her shoulder. Then the person who must be Rosa Sanchez—a chunky middle-aged woman with long curly hair dyed jet black, a tight navy blazer over jeans, a little too much makeup, and an air of authority despite her diminutive size. Teresa led the man and the camerawoman to the area between the pews and altar where she had placed four chairs and said, "You can set up here." The crew looked to Rosa Sanchez for confirmation and she nodded.

Teresa took Rosa's elbow and steered her toward the prioress. Catherine noticed the eyes first. They were large and such a dark brown that they looked almost black. Bits of makeup had collected in the tiny crow's feet, but Rosa's smile was wide and warm as she extended her hand.

"Wonderful to meet you, Sister Catherine."

"Please, just Catherine. And welcome."

"Thank you for having us. Teresa's told me all about your wonderful Sister Mary Margaret."

"Yes, she's a wonder. We're all very fond of her."

Rosa nodded noncommittally and turned back to where the crew was setting up. "Excuse me, I'll just make sure we're ready to go."

Catherine looked at Teresa. She had the air of a frightened rabbit high on amphetamines, and kept clutching at her hands.

"Stop that," Catherine said softly, laying a hand on the frenetic fingers. "Everything will be fine. Is Mary Margaret okay?"

"I think so. She was good when I left her. I can go get her now. Shall I go get her? What do you think?"

"Take a breath." Teresa took a deep breath. "You can do this." Teresa nodded. Catherine leaned in and said quietly, "I'm going to ask you one last time not to say anything about the spiritual center." Teresa frowned and pulled back.

"But why? We'd be wasting..."

"We're not going to do it. If you say we are, you'll just look foolish. And open us up to even more criticism. Stick with the Mary Margaret issue. Let's get this thing behind us." Teresa frowned and looked up at her defiantly. Catherine did not like this new game in which she was a player and not the referee, but she realized that if she pushed any harder at this point, Teresa would feel bulldozed and defensive—and fight back even harder. Teresa stared another moment, then turned away slowly and strode out of the chapel.

Catherine moved toward the TV people, now fully engaged in setting up their contraptions: a bank of lights that Catherine hoped wouldn't blow a fuse, some mysterious black boxes on the floor, tiny spider-like devices, presumably microphones, that the burly guy had twisted among his fingers.

She stood silently on the periphery until Rosa Sanchez turned and came toward her.

"So we have you, and..." She looked at her notepad. "A Sister Gemma?"

"Right. There's Sister Gemma now." She indicated the tall, aubergine-clad figure that had just entered the chapel and was hovering near the door.

"And Sister Mary Margaret?"

"Sister Teresa's gone to get her." Catherine offered her most gracious smile. "I think you'll see how deep her faith is, and how committed she is to helping people. That's what I hope people take away from this interview." Rosa narrowed her eyes slightly but kept her smile in place and nodded.

Catherine called Gemma over and introduced her to Rosa just as Teresa returned with Mary Margaret in tow. Catherine placed a hand under Mary Margaret's elbow.

"This is Sister Mary Margaret. Sister, Rosa Sanchez."

Mary Margaret raised herself to her full height, which was not very high but which Catherine thought created an elegant and authoritative air. She took Rosa's hand in both of hers and gazed into her eyes with the saintly smile that had become her trademark on Facebook. Catherine would have bet the whole convent on Mary Margaret at that moment, but then it occurred to her that she had already done so.

"It's wonderful to meet you, Rosa," Mary Margaret said, enveloping the guest in her warm glow.

"You, too, Sister. Why don't you sit right here?" Rosa seemed afraid to touch Mary Margaret at first, but then gently guided her to the center chair. Rosa sat opposite her and indicated the two seats behind Mary Margaret for Catherine and Gemma. The burly man miked up everyone. A loud *thunck*, and two large rectangles of light sprung to life, spotlighting Mary Margaret and Rosa. Catherine thought they destroyed the sacredness of the environment, but Mary Margaret didn't seem to mind at all. Teresa stood in the shadows, behind Rosa, wringing her hands.

"Ready?" Rosa asked Mary Margaret.

"Whenever you are, dear."

Rosa signaled the tattooed woman and after a slight pause, spoke to the camera. "We're here today with Sister Mary Margaret, the San Francisco nun who has become an internet sensation with posts about her conversations with God, and her message that we are all God. Welcome, Sister." The camera panned back to include the whole group. "And you have with you today your prioress, Sister Catherine, and also Sister Gemma. Are they here to protect you?"

Mary Margaret grinned good-naturedly. "Well, Rosa, you might say they're my entourage. I don't take them everywhere, mind you," she added impishly. My God, Catherine thought, she's like Betty White. Irresistible.

"Now Sister, tell me about all of us being God."

"Well first, Rosa, thank you for having me. My message is really so simple. Perhaps that's why people get confused and make it sound sensational. We all just want to know and love our God, whether we call that god Universal Mind, or Source, or even The Force. Why is that? I think it's because there is a bit of God in all of us. A divine spark, if you will. And I believe we are meant to find that spark and nurture it. That's why I've reached out to people."

Teresa, the proud coach, mouthed the words as Mary Margaret spoke them. It all seemed to be going to plan, Catherine thought.

"And your conversations with God? What is that like?" Rosa asked.

"I believe we all talk with God in our own ways, Rosa. Through intuition, through the love of our family and friends, through those little messages that come to us throughout the day. They prompt us and help us. My intuition has been to spread the word about that divine spark."

The words were just right, and she was delivering them perfectly. Catherine wondered glumly why Mary Margaret couldn't have used those same calming, reassuring words on Facebook, or with Conlon, and saved them all a lot of trouble. Of course back then, she hadn't had the benefit of Teresa's tutelage. Standing behind Rosa, Teresa seemed visibly relieved at Mary Margaret's performance. At least she'd stopped wringing her hands.

Rosa leaned back, narrowed her eyes slightly, and smiled in a way that seemed a bit patronizing, as if she didn't quite believe what she was hearing. Had Mary Margaret poked a tiger with her deft and even inspiring answers? Would Rosa feel like she had to hit back?

"But Sister, not everybody feels that divine spark. Are you telling them that they are God anyway?"

Mary Margaret stared at her, expressionless. "Everyone is God."

"But if you're God, and I'm God, what if I want it sunny and you want it to rain?"

Something was happening to Mary Margaret. She was beginning to slide around on the wide, somewhat treacherous psychological spectrum on which she operated—slipping precipitously toward the crazy end. Catherine watched as Mary Margaret sank down low in her chair, stared at the floor, and spoke almost to herself. "It's not about rain."

"Well, how does it work then, Sister? Because I don't see myself as God." Rosa smiled and leaned in. Catherine noted that as Rosa's words became harsher, her demeanor became softer and friendlier—a device she recognized from her own repertoire. Mary Margaret slowly raised her eyes and met the reporter's gaze.

"You have to surrender," Mary Margaret said, sitting up straighter and gaining steam as she spoke. "You have to let go of your human self to feel the Divine!" Oh no, Catherine thought. Do not go there. She thought of the thousands of people tuning in randomly at 7:00, expecting to hear the news of the day and instead being exhorted to abandon their human selves. But Mary Margaret was on a roll. "Abandon your ego! You're not a reporter. You're not even a woman!" Rosa's eyes flashed, but she said nothing. Catherine watched with cobra fascination as, to her horror, a wave of evangelism swept over Mary Margaret. "You're not all those fancy things you think you are—your hair, your makeup, all your 'special' feelings. When you take those things away and you're *down to your essence*, then *you are God*." Catherine started to stand and intervene, but Mary Margaret was already on her feet. The old nun raised a hand above Rosa's head. "You are! You know you are! You are risen!" Then suddenly, Mary Margaret crumpled into a heap, clutching her chest.

Rosa's mouth flew open in shock, but she glanced quickly at the camerawoman, then deliberately at Mary Margaret. The camera moved down toward the old nun. Catherine jumped up and called to Sister Jeanne, who was standing frozen in the back of the chapel, to call 911. She whirled around to the camerawoman and snapped, "Stop that!" The tattooed flattop woman turned off the camera and sheepishly lowered it to the floor as Catherine bent over Mary Margaret. She gently slapped the ancient cheek but got no response. Checked for a pulse but wasn't exactly sure where to put her fingers so wasn't too alarmed when she found none. Teresa pulled Rosa off to the side and the two began talking in hushed, urgent tones. Gemma crouched down beside Catherine.

"What can I do?" Gemma asked.

Catherine grabbed her hand and whispered, "I'm going with her to the hospital. You stay here and talk to Sanchez. Ask if you can go on camera and explain about Mary Margaret. She's elderly, the spirit moves strongly in her... You'll know what to say. I trust you." Gemma nodded.

As word of the incident spread through the convent, nuns began to converge on the chapel. One by one, they slid into the front pews and kept a respectful watch. Ten minutes later, the paramedics rushed in, got Mary Margaret onto a stretcher, and hustled her out. At the door, Catherine turned back for a final look at the ill-fated interview. The last thing she saw before turning to follow the paramedics was Teresa sitting down in Mary Margaret's chair and getting miked up.

Out on the street, a young EMT helped Catherine scramble into the back of the ambulance. "Up you go, Sister," she said, indicating a seat over to the side, out of the way. Young people in uniforms were doing CPR and squeezing an ambu bag, trying to resuscitate Mary Margaret, who now had tubes and wires coming out of her in all directions. Catherine craned around them, trying to get a look at Mary Margaret. She was ashen.

At the hospital, they whisked Mary Margaret away. Catherine fell into a chair and tried to collect herself. The ER waiting room felt smaller, more claustrophobic than it had a few days earlier. The same motel print of the small boat with a red-brown sail, but this time Catherine knew that those silver-rimmed grey clouds were about to throw down a storm. Pale lilac walls; *People*, *Newsweek*, and *Health* magazines; a TV mounted in the corner with the news yammering away. Catherine stared at it blankly. She called Gemma to find out what was happening but it went to voicemail. Thought about calling again, but didn't. She couldn't take in any more.

After about an hour, a tall doctor with a shock of grey hair and a kind face appeared.

"Sister Catherine?" She stood and nodded. "I'm Dr. Rosen. Sister Mary Margaret suffered a heart attack. A serious one. Are you aware of her medical directive?"

What did that mean? Should she know about it? "No, I don't think so."

"She has a DNR, and wants no intervention of any kind. We might operate under normal circumstances, although it would be very iffy at her age—but with this directive, we can only make her comfortable and hope for the best."

"But will she be okay?"

He paused. "We can hope for the best, but…"

"Can I see her?"

"Of course." He led her back through a maze of pale green corridors into a small sterile-looking room.

Mary Margaret lay flat on her back and seemed only partially conscious. Catherine started to reach for her hand, but Mary Margaret's arm was a maze of needles, plastic tubes, and tape and she was afraid of disturbing something. Instead, she lay her hand on the blanket next to Mary Margaret's. The wrinkled, heavily veined hand moved. Then moved again. Mary Margaret turned her head slowly from side to side and seemed to be waking up.

"Mary Margaret?"

Her eyes looked ancient, with folds Catherine had never noticed before, and her parchment skin was nearly grey. But she was rousing herself, and finally focused on Catherine. The hand reached over and covered Catherine's, then squeezed it weakly.

Mary Margaret stared at her a moment, then said in a low, husky voice, "I made a mess, didn't I?"

"No, you did a good job. People felt God in you. You helped people. Don't worry about Rosa Sanchez."

Mary Margaret looked doubtful. She shook her head and looked up toward the ceiling, then back at Catherine.

"I'm sorry."

"Don't be. Everything is fine."

Mary Margaret seemed to be studying her. "You look sad. I worry about you."

"I'm fine." She smiled, hoping to look reassuring. But as Mary Margaret continued to watch her, she felt the smile fade.

"You know what Teresa's planning?" the old nun asked. Catherine nodded. "She was talking it up to everyone while you were gone."

"I'm not surprised."

"I mean, to *everyone*. A lot."

Catherine shrugged as if it were nothing to worry about. "I've told her no. We won't be doing that."

Mary Margaret's eyes widened. "You may not have a choice." Catherine shrugged and shook her head. This was not the time to push back on Mary Margaret.

The old nun looked up at the ceiling again, and Catherine thought she might actually be seeing something up there. They sat in silence for a moment, then Mary Margaret sighed and started drumming her fingers on her stomach. She turned to Catherine and said, "I'm getting out of Dodge. You should, too." Did Mary Margaret want her to die? Or just abandon the convent to Teresa?

"What do you mean?" Catherine tried to keep her voice steady. Could Mary Margaret see into the future, now that she'd had a couple brushes with the Infinite?

"You need to stop playing nun. Find something better to do. You could be Julian's pickleball partner. Or sail around the world. Or write your sex books under your own name..." Catherine's eyebrows flew up. "Oh, I know all about Lacy Dominion. Your *nom de plume*!" She smiled slyly.

"How did you...?"

"Oh, I have my ways. You're not the only smarty-pants." Mary Margaret flicked a piece of lint off her blanket, then glanced up at Catherine. "You leave your computer lying around your office all the time. God said it would be okay if I used it to practice." She stared at Catherine, pursed her lips, and whispered, "You should have a password."

Catherine wondered what had happened to the barely conscious old woman who, just moments ago, had appeared to be dying before her eyes. She did leave her computer "lying around" her office, figuring nobody would dare... She imagined Mary Margaret skulking into the office when they were all at Chapel, having once more feigned illness and asked to be excused. And where had this sudden burst of energy come from? She had heard somewhere that right before people died, they often had a miraculous rally and appeared to be almost fully recovered. And then, having expended that last surge of life, they simply died.

"I can see that," Catherine said slowly. "I'm definitely not the only smarty pants." As long as Mary Margaret already seemed to have a few lines of communication open into the Infinite, maybe she should tap into it. "I plan to stay and make the convent stronger. Up the ante, get us back on a deeper path. Why should I, as you say, get out of Dodge?"

Mary Margaret's eyes came alive and fixed on her. "Because God wants you to be happy, and you're not happy here. Maybe not anywhere..."

Catherine tried not to wince. That was her greatest fear, that her inability to live within Spirit would follow her wherever she went. That it wasn't just the lax state of the convent or some temporary laziness that kept her from God, but some deeper failing within herself.

Mary Margaret looked tired now, and seemed to sink deeper into the pillow. The sass had gone out of her. "Nobody's indispensable. If you leave, someone will fill the gap. Like water." Then, after once more consulting the ceiling, "I don't like Rosa Sanchez."

"She was mean to you."

"No, she was mean to God." The energy began to drain out of Mary Margaret. Catherine could almost see it dissipating. Her hands went limp, but she turned her head toward Catherine and smiled. "You have to let it all go." Catherine couldn't tell if Mary Margaret was talking about her letting go of running the convent, or about herself as she let go of life.

Slowly, Mary Margaret's face went slack. The monitor shifted from weak, erratic beats to a flat tone. Catherine had heard how you could feel a person's presence leave when they died. In that moment, she knew that Mary Margaret was no longer in the room.

Two nurses and Dr. Rosen rushed in and gave her tight, sympathetic smiles. They began checking the machines, then Mary Margaret's eyes, pulse, heart, and respiration. Catherine knew what they would find, and didn't want to stay for the "pronouncement."

*

She made her way back to the waiting room, lowered herself into a chair, and stared at the TV droning on in the corner. Her mind felt blank and grey. After a few minutes, she recognized something familiar on the screen. Rosa Sanchez stood outside the convent with a microphone in her hand. On the other side of the split screen was the 7:00 news anchor, Raimunda Ramirez, her long dark hair falling over the shoulders of her red blazer.

"Today our Rosa Sanchez sat down with the now-famous San Francisco nun, Sister Mary Margaret, who claims to have visions of God. Rosa?" Catherine gripped the arms of the chair and leaned forward.

"Thanks, Raimunda," Rosa said to the camera with her big TV smile. "Yes, I'm here at the convent without a name, the No Name Convent, a loose affiliation of women seeking to live a life of quiet contemplation here on Fulton Street in San Francisco."

Catherine took heart. So far, so good. She reminded herself to breathe.

"I sat down in the convent chapel with Sister Mary Margaret and two of the sisters she calls 'her entourage'..."

The screen shifted to the recorded interview in the chapel. There they were. Mary Margaret up front looking friendly and benign, reciting the rote answers that Teresa had given her. For a second, Catherine didn't recognize herself as the woman sitting next to Gemma in the background. Did she really look that old? She had been trying to look serene and wise, but on the screen she looked grim and anxious. Gemma looked quietly joyous. The camera liked her.

Rosa was asking the question about what would happen if she were God and wanted it sunny, and Mary Margaret were God and wanted it to rain. Mary Margaret suddenly turned stiff, then sank down so far in her chair that Catherine thought she might fall out of the camera's frame. At the time, sitting behind Mary Margaret, she hadn't been able to see the old nun's face. She looked...surly. "It's not about rain," Mary Margaret mumbled to the floor. And then, oh God, the rant about how Rosa would have to surrender her ego and stop being her human self. Not be a reporter, or a woman, or care about her "special" feelings or her hair. Why hadn't Teresa prepared Mary Margaret for that question? Giving up your ego was a bad topic for the 7:00 TV-tray audience. Had Mary Margaret really said that about Rosa's hair?

Catherine watched herself sit in a catatonic stupor as Mary Margaret began to slide off the rails. Why hadn't she jumped in and rephrased everything on the spot? Why had she just sat there? Even Gemma looked a little wild-eyed as she stole a glance at Catherine, then returned her gaze to Mary Margaret, who was now on her feet with a hand over Rosa's head, crying, "You are! You know you are! You are risen!" Catherine steeled herself for the part where Mary Margaret collapsed—but it never came.

Instead, they cut back to Rosa standing outside the convent. "Right after Sister gave me that blessing, Raimunda, what I now call 'The Risen Blessing,' she was taken ill. One of her entourage attended to her and we completed the interview with the convent's spokesperson, Sister Teresa, and their spiritual director, Sister Gemma."

Spokesperson? Spiritual director? *She* was the convent's spiritual director! Was Gemma in on this?

The scene flipped back to the chapel. Teresa was in Mary Margaret's chair, and Gemma's chair had been moved up next to her so that they were sitting side-by-side. Catherine's chair had been removed entirely. Rosa smiled into the camera.

"Sister Teresa and Sister Gemma. Welcome!"

Catherine stood and moved toward the TV. It was Teresa who answered the reporter, of course.

"Thank you, Rosa. Sister Mary Margaret has had so many demands on her time lately, I'm afraid she's missed her nap the past few days. Thanks for the opportunity to expand on the wisdom she gave us earlier." Rosa nodded pleasantly. Teresa shifted in her seat, leaned forward, and said partly to Rosa, partly to the camera, "When Sister talks about all of us being God, she means that we all share a spark of the Divine—and that it's our birthright to discover and enjoy that spark. When she says we are risen, she means that we all can transcend our human problems and find that divine peace, love, and joy in ourselves and one another.

"I see," Rosa said dryly. "And what is this place, really? I mean, are you Catholic?" Teresa turned to Gemma.

"We aren't associated with any formal religion," Gemma said smoothly, in a much friendlier way than Catherine had ever seen her speak. Who knew she would have such a knack for this kind of thing? "We've come together to live a quiet, prayerful life. To meditate for peace and understanding around the world." She was such an appealing presence that it was easy to believe anything she said. No sooner had Gemma stopped speaking than Teresa piped up again.

"We're so grateful to Sister Mary Margaret for letting people know about us, because we'll be going out into the community now and sharing what we've learned. We'll be offering retreats, classes, and meditation groups. We hope you'll come back, Rosa, when we start launching these programs."

Rosa nodded and said, "Thank you for spending some time with us, Sisters." She turned toward the camera and said graciously, "This is Rosa Sanchez, reporting from the No Name Convent in San Francisco."

And suddenly, they were back in the studio and Raimunda Ramirez was saying, "Thanks, Rosa. We'll have the weekend weather when we return. Don't go anywhere." A commercial for dishwasher soap pods began.

Catherine felt a little dizzy and sat back down. Could this be happening? Total mutiny, possibly including even Gemma? She had better get back there right away and put down this thing before it got completely out of hand. When the others heard her vision of a deeper spirituality and a more focused day-to-day life, they would certainly fall in line behind her. Teresa would have to back down. Or leave.

Dr. Rosen appeared and sat down next to her. "I'm so sorry," he said. Catherine nodded, feeling tears in her eyes. Rosen handed her a large clear plastic bag containing Mary Margaret's effects. Catherine could see bits of her aubergine robe, shoes, socks, a watch.

"Sister Mary Margaret left instructions last time she was here. She asked to be cremated, and for the ashes to be sent back to her sister in Indiana. Terra Haute? Did you know about this?" Catherine shook her head. She hadn't known about anything. "The Neptune Society is handling it."

She nodded. "Thank you, Doctor." Catherine watched him move away down the corridor, his hands jammed into the pockets of his white coat, looking a little stooped.

She felt stooped, too, but gathered herself and the plastic bag and strode through the maze of pale green corridors to the sunny lobby and the street.

CHAPTER FOURTEEN

TIPPING POINT

The hospital was only a few blocks from the convent, and Catherine chose a path through the park rather than the Fulton Street sidewalk. What was waiting for her back there, now that Teresa had formally announced the spiritual center on TV? Hopefully, the others would either ignore or reject the idea, and nothing would come of it—leaving the path open for her more rigorous program. Perhaps, after a decent interval, she could even link the new program to Mary Margaret's passing. "She showed us the way with her devotion and commitment. Surely, she would want that deeper connection for all of us…" The sharp scent of eucalyptus braced her. She looked up and drew strength from the dark green canopy of Monterey pines against a bright blue sky.

The trail came out of the park right across the street from the convent. Catherine thought of Rosa Sanchez standing out in front, telling the world about them. The place felt more public already. She imagined Teresa putting up an orange neon sign: "Open for business!" Then quickly banished the thought. She checked her watch. They would just be finishing dinner.

As she pushed through the front door into the entryway, she heard Teresa's voice. "Finally, we can share everything we've learned with the world. It will be..." She rounded the corner into the living room and saw them all standing at the foot of the staircase, with Teresa a few steps up. Some grinned broadly at the vision she was laying before them. Others smiled politely. Still others looked confused. Catherine stopped, and they all turned toward her. Now a few of them actually looked frightened. She let the silence extend a few beats, and then stepped forward.

"Sisters, I have sad news. Our dear Mary Margaret has gone to her God." Murmurs of shock and sorrow. "Our meditation tonight will be a remembrance of her." Then, in a voice styled to be both calm and friendly, "Sister Teresa, may I see you before Chapel? In about a half hour?" They parted to let her pass, wide-eyed and silent. Some smiled tentatively at her, others looked at the floor. She moved past Teresa and up the stairs with a tight smile.

Safe in her room, she collapsed onto her bed, glad that she'd had the presence of mind to give herself some time before talking to Teresa.

A knock on the door. Who on Earth? She pulled herself up and opened the door a crack. Gemma. Gemma, who had sat next to Teresa as she'd pitched the spiritual center on TV.

"What can I do for you, Sister?"

"You can let me in, and talk to me."

So. No more courtesies to the prioress, apparently. That might be just as well. She wanted an accurate lay of the land, and Gemma probably had it. She opened the door and stood aside. Gemma glided in and took a seat on the bed. She sighed and looked up at Catherine. "You've had quite a day." Catherine nodded and sat down next to her. "How was it at the hospital?"

"Hard." She paused. "Easy." She thought again. "I don't know." Gemma patted her hand.

"It's about to get worse," Gemma said. "Uh, Teresa talked about the spiritual center thing on TV. And again at dinner. She's making quite a pitch." From the careful way she was presenting this information, Catherine guessed that Gemma knew all about the conflict over the spiritual center.

"What do people think?" Catherine tried to look arch and unaffected, but suspected she wasn't fooling Gemma.

"She's been working people pretty hard, even before today apparently. Making promises. Painting pictures of an easier life. More engaged with folks beyond our walls." She paused and looked at the floor. "More fun." That smarted. Had Gemma gone over to the carnival side?

"You're with her on this?"

Gemma waved away the question. "I want everyone to be happy."

Catherine sat up straighter. "Strange. When I was up in Sonoma, I had just the opposite vision. I want us to go deeper. Be quieter, more focused on the invisible Reality, the mysteries." That would hook Gemma, surely.

Gemma nodded. "Right. Just the opposite of what Teresa's saying," she said softly. After a moment of silence Gemma ventured, "I think people may be tired of the quiet."

"But that's just when we should dig deeper," Catherine insisted. "Resistance is part of the journey. It's there so we can learn to press beyond it."

"I see what you're saying." Gemma carefully. "But I don't think they're there."

"What's she saying that has everyone so excited?"

"She talks about people coming here, thinking we're wonderful, even guru-ish. Like the Ananda Center but with robes. Mary Pat will do the animal thing. Heather the sacred feminine. Like that."

"What about you?"

Gemma looked down at the bedspread. "Meditation."

"That, I can see. But the rest of it is just frivolous." Catherine couldn't hold back her exasperation. "Unserious! *Crazy.*"

"I don't know. You could teach writing..." Catherine flushed. Did everyone know about Lacy Dominion? Had Mary Margaret entertained everyone with gossip about the bodice-rippers? "Or administration!" Gemma corrected herself. "Or maybe business..." Her voice trailed off under Catherine's withering look.

"This has to stop. I'll get the whole thing straightened out tonight at Chapel." She stood and tried to speak calmly. She didn't want to jeopardize her connection with Gemma. "Thank you for the information. I appreciate it." She hesitated and considered asking for Gemma's support, but Gemma was looking at the floor. "See you tonight." She opened the door. Gemma squeezed her hand on the way out.

Catherine stood staring at the door. This was going to be harder than she'd anticipated. A lot harder. If she'd lost Gemma... Clearly, she couldn't wait to present her new program. Teresa's plan wouldn't be knocked down easily. She would have to engage it directly. And immediately.

Another rap on the door, and little Sister Jeanne stood holding a tray with a large white napkin draped over it.

"I'm sorry. I don't mean to disturb..."

"Oh no, come in," Catherine said smoothly. Jeanne crept in, not raising her eyes from the white napkin, and muttered, "I made a tray in case you were hungry. Since you missed dinner. I'll just leave it here." She set the tray down on the desk. "So sorry to..."

"Thank you! That was very thoughtful of you. Did you make it yourself?" Catherine peeked under the napkin.

"Um, yes. Kale Shepherd's Pie," Jeanne said with a proud smile, glancing up at Catherine.

"Ah. Kale." Jeanne turned to go but Catherine stopped her. "Sister, may I ask a favor of you?"

"Of course!" Jeanne seemed to come to life. Catherine picked up the plastic bag containing Mary Margaret's things and held them to her chest for a moment.

"These are Sister Mary Margaret's effects. I don't really know what to do with them. But you will, I believe. Will you take them, please, and do what you think best?"

Jeanne stared at the plastic bag as if it were a saint's relic, then slowly extended both hands, palms up, to receive it. Catherine placed the bag into her hands, trying to mirror her reverence. Finally, Jeanne said, "I'll launder everything and find a lovely box for it. In time, we'll know if anything else is to be done." Catherine felt herself soften. She never would have thought of that, but it came naturally to Jeanne. And the little nun had braved the lion's den to bring her dinner.

"Thank you, Sister. That would be perfect. I trust you completely."

Jeanne beamed up at her, backing toward the door as she said more loudly than Catherine had ever heard her speak, "Thank you!" And slid away into the corridor.

*

After Catherine had glided past them up the staircase, Teresa gave the group a conspiratorial smile and a quiet "More later!" then turned and retreated to her room. There, she began pacing and replaying the encounter with Catherine. Not a confrontation, really. Just the first time they had been under the same roof since Teresa had gone public about the spiritual center—in flagrant defiance of Catherine's wishes. The sight of her coming around that corner from the vestibule had made Teresa's heart stop! She had felt queasy ever since. Third chakra stuff! The seat of self-esteem, will, confidence, and movement from inertia into action. Well, that was no surprise. She'd been working her third chakra overtime, running on adrenalin for the past twenty-four hours, stepping into her power! But OMG, what if Catherine struck back at her? Should she just pack her things now, in case Catherine got the rest of them to banish her, and head for the Valley? No. She had to see this through. Besides, the Valley wasn't exactly rushing to embrace her.

To calm and energize her third chakra, she took a deep, cleansing breath and struck a yoga pose that Sanjay at the Ananda Center had taught her. "Warrior"—lunging forward with her arms extended above her head. She held the pose for a few moments, then moved slowly out of it and looked in the mirror. It was time for a change around this place, and that change had her name on it. OMG, time! She was almost late for Catherine. How had that whole half hour slipped away?

She paused at Catherine's door, remembering the day when she had stood trembling outside the prioress's office, determined to beg for the right to do the convent's books. She would never have dared knock on the prioress's bedroom door back then. Awesome progress! She calibrated her knock to be clear, confident, even collegial. After what seemed like minutes, the door opened. Catherine stood before her, smiling a little stiffly, her head tilted back and to the side. As if she were examining an insect, Teresa thought. She said as smoothly as she could, "Hello...Catherine."

"Come in." The prioress didn't seem angry. Was that a good sign or a bad sign? "Have a seat." Teresa sat gingerly on the bed. Catherine pulled over the little desk chair and sat facing her. She leaned forward, elbows on her knees, and looked at Teresa. "Thank you for coming," she said softly.

Teresa willed her fingers to be still and focused all her energy on anticipating Catherine's tricks. Like this one, pretending to be grateful that she had come, when Catherine had ordered her to do so. She gave the prioress a tight smile and lifted her chin. Catherine leaned back in her chair and asked, "How have the past few days been for you?" Was this a trap? Did she really want to know? Would she use the information as a weapon? This was three-dimensional chess. She decided on the one course of action that was consistently working for her: telling the truth.

"It's been challenging. Uncomfortable. Scary. But something's pushing me forward."

Catherine nodded. "I know the feeling."

"You do?" Could this be true? That Catherine felt uncomfortable?

"Of course. Do you think it's any fun to be in my position?" Teresa looked away, focused on the lone tapered candle on the desk. Her gut told her Catherine was being honest. In a way, that was harder to deal with than the chess game.

"What position is that?" Even as she spoke, Teresa realized that this was just the sort of parry Catherine would use.

"Well...to an outsider, this might look like we're in a power struggle," Catherine said pleasantly. "Except I'm not struggling." The prioress leaned in a bit more. "But you are." Teresa felt as if she'd been struck by a bolt of lightning. "You know where you want to be, but you're not strong enough to get there."

Teresa pulled herself out of the paralysis. "Yes, I am. I know what I'm doing. People are with me." Catherine shook her head slightly and leaned back in her chair.

"Here's what I propose," she said, acting as if she were about to outline the only rational path. "Tonight I'm going to lay out my vision for us. We will be quieter, deeper, more focused inward. We'll nurture a more stable, solid, intimate relationship with the Divine. If you stick with me, I'll teach you how to run this place. And in a few years, who knows? When you're in charge, you can do whatever you want."

Teresa could not believe what she'd just heard. Catherine's vision was exactly the opposite of hers. Precisely the wrong direction. And she didn't believe for a minute that Catherine would turn the convent over to her "in a few years."

"We'll start the day at 5:00 with an hour of meditation, then some free time before breakfast, which will be silent." To Teresa the thought of silence and inwardness felt like prison. "Then chores, another meditation, and lunch. In the afternoon, we'll read and discuss spiritual books, then more meditation and..."

Teresa would die if they went in that direction. She could not allow it! And unlike Catherine, she had been building a base of support among the sisters. They were excited about using their talents in the service of others. She could get her way.

"That's not going to happen," she said in a low, steady voice.

"Oh, Sister," Catherine shot back. "It most certainly is."

Teresa stood and looked down at Catherine, hoping to convey an impression of calm superiority—then turned on her heel and made herself walk, not run, from the room.

CHAPTER FIFTEEN

SMACKDOWN IN THE CHAPEL

Catherine stared at the door after Teresa left. She hadn't expected so much *will* from the younger woman. The force of it had surprised her. She would need to stand strong and clear before the others tonight, and lay out her vision in an irresistible way. She had never before needed to bring so much of herself to swaying this rather compliant group. But swaying was her specialty, she reminded herself.

She checked her watch. Five minutes until 8:00 Chapel. She wrapped herself in the prioress glamour and moved into the corridor, down the stairs, and to the front of the chapel where, only hours earlier, Teresa had sat and announced to the world that they were open for business. The others filed in slowly and filled the first two rows.

Catherine centered herself, smiled graciously at the group, and gathered them into her thrall.

"My dear sisters, we have all suffered a terrible loss today. In a few days we will have a formal service to commemorate our dear Sister Mary Margaret's passing...so just a few words about her tonight. She was, in many ways, the heart of our community. The depth of her faith, her openness to God, and her spirit of service will be much missed. And yet, we know that she is in her glory now. She is home, watching us and guiding us with love.

"I was honored to accompany her on her last journey, and to hear again her message that we are all One in God. I have been thinking long and hard since Sister's final moments, and realize that I have become lax in pursuing that most important treasure, intimacy with God. I've been distracted by worldly things, and not devoted my full energy to the only pursuit that really matters—living in an abundant and ever-increasing closeness with the Divine. That is how Mary Margaret lived, and she set an example for all of us.

"To that end, I invite you to join me in a renewal of that spiritual quest. I see for us a deeper commitment to meditation, to silence, to listening to the wisdom of those who came before us on the path. I propose that we put together a new schedule that focuses on contemplation, on silence, on the Inward Eye that reveals who we truly are. That, after all, is why we first came together."

There it was. That was what she wanted. She paused and looked around the room. The expressions ranged from blank, to bored, to confused, to agitated. Not what she had hoped for or expected. She had felt a disquiet among them as she was speaking, and it became even more evident when she stopped. People exchanged glances, and several seemed to be trying to catch Teresa's eye.

Gemma raised her hand. "What would this look like?" Catherine was relieved to have some interaction, and a specific question to answer.

"I think perhaps we should start with three hour-long Chapel meditations a day—morning, mid-day, and evening—and a few more hours of silence. Perhaps a little less time outside our walls."

She didn't like how she sounded—schoolmarmish. It felt as if they had all stopped breathing and solidified into a huge block of resistance. Nobody was smiling. Or jumping in. Finally, Teresa raised her hand. Catherine nodded and Teresa stood.

"Is this set in stone? I mean, do we even get to vote?" She sounded earnest, but it was clearly a challenge. Catherine smiled as warmly as she could.

"Of course, nothing is set in stone. We're a community. No one's imposing anything. We'll all help find our path forward." Teresa turned her attention to the group.

"Well, as some of you know, I've had another idea." As she spoke, Teresa moved slowly up the aisle to stand next to Catherine. It felt like an assault, and Catherine stepped slightly to the side. "It's possible that God wants us to go *out*, not *in*. To contribute, rather than to hoard. To share, rather than to focus only on ourselves. Our spiritual center would be a chance to do all those things. To develop our talents and offer them to the world. What we've done up to now has been good, but I think it's time for a new energy, a new focus. It's time for us to *wake up*," she said with a broad smile, which many in the audience returned. They were with her, Catherine saw. "Wake up and *smell the coffee!*" A wave of laughter. A few still seemed uncertain, and little Sister Jeanne's eyes kept darting back and forth between her and Teresa. A few cast her pitying glances as if she had already been vanquished.

"What do you think?" Teresa asked the group. They seemed hesitant at first. Did they feel guilty? Relieved to have an alternative to her stiff regimen? After a moment, Mary Pat's hand went up. Teresa nodded to her, and they all swiveled around as Mary Pat stood at the far end of the second row.

"Hey, I'm all about God. But you know, also God's creatures. Sometimes being with Scat makes me feel closer to God. I could tell people about that. The Episcopalians have a 'Blessing of the Animals' service. We could do that. People could bring... I mean, I'm all for meditation." She glanced briefly at Catherine with a half-hearted smile. "But you know, other things, too."

"Thank you, Sister," Teresa beamed. "Anyone else?" Jeanne half raised her hand. "Yes! Sister Jeanne."

Jeanne didn't stand, or even look up, but for once she spoke so clearly that everyone could hear her. "Bread is holy. Baking is holy. We honor God by taking care of others." They stared for a moment. A few nodded solemnly, then looked back to Teresa.

Julian stood without being recognized. "I don't know about you, but I don't think I could stay if we're just going to meditate and read more. I gotta get out." With that, she plopped back down on the hard wooden pew. A few looked askance at her, but others nodded.

"Understood," Teresa said almost under her breath. "Who else?"

Catherine thought she might get some support from Heather, who had been squirming in her seat, but the witch turned to Jeanne, who was sitting next to her, and said loudly

enough that everyone could hear, "I'm with the pickleballer."
A wave of nervous laughter.

Catherine looked desperately at Gemma and finally, Gemma raised her hand. She rarely spoke, so all eyes turned to her.

"I have loved our years of quiet contemplation and prayer, and I'm grateful to Sister Catherine for leading us through that passage. But I think we can come close to God in many ways, and sometimes it's good to try new things."

Catherine felt her shoulders slump. Teresa gave her a triumphant look, and Catherine returned it with a stiff smile as she stepped to the center again and Teresa returned to her seat. She had lost. They had turned on her. To press further would only make it worse. How had she not known this would happen? After all she had given to them, all she had stood for…and they were just tossing her aside. She reasoned that maybe they just wanted a softer, easier way—but it felt personal.

"Thank you for your thoughts, sisters," she said without letting her voice waver. Maybe she could cover the situation with gentle humor. "I see which way the wind is blowing." She said it with more generosity than she felt, and that elicited a wave of smiles that seemed sympathetic, if not enthusiastic. "I'll take all this under advisement and let you know tomorrow morning at Chapel where we go from here. Why don't we sit in meditation, just for a half hour, and then go to bed. It's been a long day."

But she didn't sit. She walked down the aisle and up the stairs to her room.

*

erine saw her hand tremble as she turned the door-
he slipped inside and sat at her desk. What had just
d? All her authority had had simply melted away under a few rather pedestrian words from Teresa. How could an idea that had seemed so right to her be so wrong for everyone else? And an idea that seemed so wrong to her seem so right for everyone else? They had been polite, but it was almost as if they felt sorry for her. As if they saw her as an obsolete old woman, without value and struggling to discipline people who had a whole different set of interests and priorities.

A knock. She didn't want to see anyone, but wanted even less for the word to go out that she was too ashamed even to answer her door. Gemma stood in the doorway, but Catherine did not invite her in.

"Don't be like that," Gemma said softly. "Let me in." Catherine stood aside.

"How could you do that? Side with her?"

Gemma sat on the bed. "I told the truth. My truth, anyway. Please believe that I'm not against you."

"In this, you are. She won, and you helped her."

Gemma patted a place next to her on the bed. "I know this hurts."

Catherine sat. "It's humiliating. Mortifying. How long has it been like this? Did you know? Why didn't you tell me?"

"This spiritual center idea has a life of its own. It wasn't mine to manage." Gemma paused, and neither woman looked at the other. "Listen. From one point of view, I know this feels awful. But from another, it could be liberating. Your prioress authority took a hit, but maybe that's a good thing. Maybe you've outgrown it."

"I don't like being usurped!"

"Of course, you don't. Nobody would. But maybe it's not being 'usurped.' Maybe it's more like being 'moved along.' And not by Teresa. By life."

"I hate it."

"I know. But you're not happy here."

Catherine shifted on the bed and looked at Gemma. "Before she died, Mary Margaret said the same thing. She told me I had to let go of all this."

Gemma nodded. "Good advice."

"Just give up everything we have and let it become a circus?"

Gemma smiled sympathetically. "I don't think it will be a circus exactly." She rose and got Catherine a tissue from the desk, then sat back down next to her.

Catherine studied the floor. "If I left, do you think Teresa could pull it off?"

"I do. I'd help her. I need to be doing something more than just sending good thoughts to Tibet." She paused and tried to stifle a smile. "Jeanne told me—in strictest confidence—that she wants to teach a course on 'The Holiness of Housework.'"

"Oh God! She's so sweet, but can you see me hawking that?"

Gemma smiled and shook her head. "No."

"But the place would go to the dogs!" Catherine said. "Wouldn't it?"

"No," Gemma said seriously. "It'd be fine. And even if it did go to the dogs, it wouldn't be your problem."

"I don't know what to do."

"That's because you still hurt too much. You'll figure it out." Gemma stood, and Catherine stood with her. "I think you should take a shower and go to bed. You'll know what to do in the morning.

Catherine nodded, even though she didn't share Gemma's confidence. "Thank you."

"You're welcome. Now get some sleep." She touched Catherine's shoulder and quietly pulled the door shut as she left.

Catherine sat back down on the bed. She knew that a good person—not herself, but a good person—would humbly accept the consensus. She would support Teresa and the spiritual center, do whatever she could to make it a success. But even on her best days, she was not that person. Her one shard of certainty was that she did not want to be a mere acolyte, a powerless figure lurking in the shadows as Teresa made all the decisions. On the other hand, she didn't want people to think she'd just given up and disappeared—a weak, humiliated nobody whom Teresa had driven into the wilderness.

She undressed, got into the shower, and let the soft hot water stream over her.

CHAPTER SIXTEEN

WAKING UP

Gemma was right. In the morning, Catherine knew exactly what to do. She didn't like it, but she knew.

There were only two choices, both bad. The first was to stay and hawk workshops for Teresa, to become an underling caught in the cacophony of yet another Consciousness Circuit sideshow, with no possibility for either intimacy with God or ego gratification. The second was to leave. She would just get in the car and go. To Sonoma. It was as good a place as any, and it had healed her in the past. She would take herself down to zero and start from scratch. Let go of everything. She could see the wisdom in that path, but it felt both dangerous and mortifying. She could put a good face on it for the convent, pretend that she was making a real choice and was happy about it—but the truth was, she felt like a pariah being banished into the desert. The banishment was humiliating, but it was better than the alternative—staying and being a monkey to Teresa's organ grinder.

A soft knock on the door, and she could feel who it was. Teresa stood with head bowed, looking at the floor. "May I come in?" Catherine stepped aside, but didn't speak. Teresa finally looked at her. "I just wanted to know where we are."

Catherine tilted her head to one side, folded her arms, and said with a steady smile, "People like your idea of the spiritual center. I think that's where we are."

Teresa grinned and clutched her hands in front of her face. "Oh, thank you! Thank *God*. I'm so relieved. It's going to be wonderful! You'll see. And I know you'll have a lot to offer, too. We'll find some exciting things for you to do." She reached over tentatively and touched Catherine's arm. "Other than run the day-to-day here, of course. You can do whatever else you..."

"Oh, I couldn't do that. You'll run everything!" Catherine said with a big, friendly smile. Teresa's grin faded.

"But..."

"You'll be great."

"But I can't do that. That's your thing."

"I don't think so," Catherine said thoughtfully, gazing out the window. "Not anymore. I want to do something different. Something new. Actually, I'm leaving."

"You can't leave!"

"Tomorrow morning."

"No! You have to stay! To run things! I can't do that."

"Of course, you can. Gemma will help you."

Teresa's face flushed. "You're trying to make me fail! Make our whole center fail!"

"No," Catherine said calmly. "I'm just ready for a change."

"You're running away!" Teresa said through clenched teeth. "Because you *lost*."

Catherine shrugged. Teresa might see through her, but she wouldn't give her the satisfaction of admitting the truth. "Think what you want, but I'm going. You'll figure it out."

Teresa's anger seemed to turn to frustration, and in a matter of seconds the frustration turned to tears.

"Listen to me," Catherine said as gently as she could. Teresa wiped her eyes and looked up. "I know you don't think you can do this, but you can. I wouldn't leave if I didn't think you could."

Teresa slumped and looked down. "I'm glad I won, but I want you here."

"You'll do fine without me."

"But I want you to show me stuff. How to handle things."

"Honestly, Teresa, I think you show great promise in 'handling things.'" Teresa glanced up at her, then she returned to pouting. "Now go. I'll give a speech in Chapel and hand the reins over to you."

"But..."

"No 'buts.' Go. I'll see you down there."

Teresa turned slowly and left—with a new onslaught of tears on the way, Catherine suspected.

Maintaining the serene, centered demeanor had been challenging, but not as difficult as she'd feared. And the encounter had been good practice for her speech in the chapel. Teresa had seemed to buy the pretense that all was well and that she was fine with leaving. For the group, she would simply maintain that same face-saving stance and add some embellishments. Adopt a breezy, positive attitude...at least until she was out of here, on the road, and could allow whatever feelings were down there to surface. Until then, they would have to stay hidden, even from herself.

*

Catherine stood in the front of the chapel, facing the other ten sisters. They seemed anxious. Tiny uncertain frowns on some of the older faces. Curiosity or intrigue on a few of the younger ones. Gemma and Teresa sat together in the front row, looking serene. Well, Gemma looked serene. Teresa was trying, but Catherine could see the effort it was taking to keep those twitching fingers still.

"Your prayers are very much appreciated at this sad time of Sister Mary Margaret's passing," Catherine began. "But as we know, every time of sorrow opens up into a time of new beginnings. Our new beginnings are very exciting, and we are going to step into those uplifting and enriching new times right away." She paused. "We can look forward to our new spiritual center, and I will be making a new personal beginning as well, answering a call to quiet and contemplation outside the city—in Sonoma. I've been thinking about this for some time, and now seems like the perfect time to start this new chapter. I'll be leaving tomorrow morning." A few gasps, which she acknowledged with a slight nod and a confident, expansive smile. "You will be in Sister Teresa's very capable hands. Her energy and enthusiasm are boundless and I know you will all support her in making a great success of our new offerings. Sister Gemma will be at her side as counselor, and you could not be better served than you will be by these two dedicated women. I want to thank each of you for all you've contributed to me over these years. I don't have the words to express my gratitude. Any questions?" The little speech seemed too short, almost curt, but she wanted to keep it simple. The more she said, the greater the odds that they would see through her.

Nobody spoke. Questions could be touchy, but no questions or answers could be even touchier. If she simply walked away after just this little set piece, it would leave them with a lot of uncertainty and loose ends—and make them suspicious that she was being ousted. She needed some interaction to make it all seem real, to them and to herself. She sighed and moved out of presentation mode, left her position at the front and stepped in among them.

"Oh, come on. You must have a million questions. I would. Yes, Sister Teresa really does have my full support. Her stepping up to these new responsibilities could not have come at a better time for me. I've felt this calling for about a year and been discerning whether or not to leave. Now both of us can move into what's next for us." That seemed to loosen the energy a little. Some shoulders went down and a few faces relaxed. Mary Pat raised her hand.

"I don't like it!" she shouted. Several of the sisters turned to stare at her. Catherine nodded.

"I understand. Change is hard, but I've thought this through and it's what I want to do. I appreciate your honesty." Mary Pat shifted in her seat and frowned, but seemed to accept the inevitable.

"Are you ill?" Heather piped up. "I know a healer who..."

"No, no, I'm not ill," Catherine said. "In fact, since I made this decision, I've never felt better. But thanks for your concern." She paused and looked around the group. "Anything else?" Some still looked uncertain, some upset, some relieved. It would take a while for this to settle, so she went on. "I want each of you to think about how you might contribute to this new era. I imagine that Sister Jeanne will be leading a course on the holiness of everyday tasks and taking care of people, and she will be wonderful." They all swiveled around to look at Jeanne, who turned beet red. Catherine began a soft little clap of appreciation and the rest followed. She nodded encouragement and resumed. "What are your gifts? What can you share with the world? I invite each of you to ponder what your contribution will be and talk with Sister Teresa about it. Questions?" Nobody raised her hand. Catherine figured she had done all that she could do, even set them on a path to getting involved with the new regime. "No? Well, I'll be around today if you want to talk. I'm buying a car this morning but I'll be back about 2:00. I'll be in the dining room if anybody wants to talk."

With that, she swept out of the chapel. As she closed the door behind her, she saw that Teresa had taken her place in the front of the room.

*

Buying a blue Honda Civic sedan proved easier than Catherine could have imagined. The aubergine robe probably dropped the price a good $1,000, and she was delighted with the deal she'd struck.

She was back at the convent by 2:00 and took a place not at the head of the long dining room table but on the side. She would hang out there, as promised, for the rest of the day in case anybody wanted to talk. For the first hour, it felt like people were avoiding her. They scurried here and there, apparently caught up in plans with Teresa for the new regime. A few gave her the side eye or a shy smile as they passed in the corridor, but most just moved more quickly when they saw her. She felt invisible in the place she had built and run for a decade, and tried to cover the shock and hurt by playing Rummikub on her phone.

Over the next hour, the post-lunch scramble abated and the place calmed down considerably. In fact, the convent took on an eerie quiet. Small noises—a snatch of conversation, a footstep, a door closing—echoed in the empty hallways, but everyone seemed to have disappeared. She looked out the window at her Monterey pines and cypress, at the eucalyptus with its soft, patchy bark and fluttering crescent leaves, and felt a tug on her heart.

A small scratch as the door from the kitchen pushed open and little Sister Jeanne crept in with another tray draped in a white napkin. She glanced shyly at Catherine as she placed the tray before her and said softly, but with obvious pride, "Scrambled eggs with chives and Jarlsberg. Your favorite." Catherine lifted the corner of the napkin for a peek and beheld a generous dollop of slightly crusted eggs cooked hard, just the way she liked them. She smiled at Jeanne, hoping to convey the child-at-Christmas delight that she felt. "And dark rye toast, with Irish butter," Jeanne added almost shyly, whisking off the napkin to reveal the full glory of her creation. Catherine patted the chair next to her, and Jeanne slid down into it.

"Thank you, Sister. This is incredibly thoughtful of you."

"You missed lunch, and I wanted you to have all your favorites before you left."

Catherine loaded her fork with eggs and chewed slowly, savoring the bite with her eyes closed. "Just delicious!" she intoned. "I'm in another realm entirely!" She took another bite as Jeanne squirmed with delight, watching her. "Really. You are so kind. Thank you, Sister." Catherine turned her attention to the dark rye toast, so saturated with butter that it practically dripped when she picked it up, and said, "Now tell me about your Holiness of Housework course..."

Jeanne blushed, but launched into what Catherine thought was a highly articulate, heartfelt description of what she wanted to share with people. Washing a coffee mug was like cleaning away anything that got in the way of experiencing the Divine within. Dusting was gently moving away any prejudices or judgments that kept her from loving other people. Laundry was cleansing one's soul and spreading light into the world. Ironing was a way to straighten the path. None of this was remotely familiar to Catherine, or even resonant with her. Yet Jeanne made it completely convincing, even appealing.

Catherine pushed the last bits of egg onto the last bite of toast and popped it into her mouth, savoring the crisp, buttery, cheesy combination. Then she turned to Jeanne and said, "I'm impressed. Not just with your ideas, but with how beautifully you present them. I'm sure your workshop will be a huge success." Jeanne ducked her head. "You may even attract a group of people who might not have been interested in the other courses." Jeanne peeked up at her and nodded, as if that were exactly what she had in mind. Independence, the last thing she expected from Jeanne. "It'll be a real service." She surprised even herself with the strength and warmth of her appreciation. She had certainly not seen all there was to see about Jeanne! "Now I know you're busy, so thank you again for the lovely meal."

Jeanne stood, picked up the tray, hesitated, then said, "Sister Catherine, thank you. You've been a model for me." Catherine could not imagine Jeanne using her as a model. In fact, it occurred to her that she might use Jeanne's kindness and thoughtfulness as a model. "May I have your blessing?" Jeanne bowed her head and appeared to be waiting for something.

Catherine had no idea what to do, or what Jeanne expected, so she simply stood, put her hand on Jeanne's bowed head, and said, "Go in peace. And love." It seemed completely inadequate, but those were the only words that came to mind and they seemed to thrill Jeanne, who looked up with a radiant smile and scurried away into the kitchen.

Catherine sat slowly and suddenly felt very alone. She was tempted to play more Rummikub to numb the feeling, but instead she just sat with it. Would she be kinder and more compassionate in Sonoma?

She glanced up at the purple and gold OM symbol she'd hung on the dining room wall—the one that Mary Margaret had accidently captured in one of her selfies. She supposed she'd hung it there in an effort to underscore that this was not necessarily a Christian place, that they had a more universal orientation. She scanned the familiar room again. Something drew her eye down to the corner, near the baseboard. A piece of sage paint was peeling away from the wall, and had taken on a pale grey tinge. She'd get Julian to... No, that wasn't her job anymore.

As if on cue, Julian appeared in the doorway from the hall, clutching a bright green book to her chest. She swung into the room with a hardy, "Hope I'm not disturbing you" and dropped into the chair next to Catherine.

"Not at all. I'm glad to have a chance to say goodbye."

Julian beamed. "I got you this. You might find it useful where you're going." She held forth the green book, *Pickleball and the Kingdom*. "There's a big pickleball community in Sonoma County." Then, conspiratorially, "They tape the pickleball court lines over the lines on the tennis courts." Julian paused, then leaned in as if to divulge the exact location of the Templars' buried treasure, "Look for the tennis courts."

"Thank you, Sister," Catherine said, holding the book with both hands in her lap. "I'll treasure this." Julian hesitated, something Catherine had never seen her do.

"Uh, one more thing," Julian said as if it had just occurred to her. Catherine smiled at the rangy nun. "The Nationals are next month. Pray for me?"

Catherine tilted her head back and followed with an exaggerated nod. "Of course! You'll definitely be in my prayers."

"Thanks!" Julian stood, patted Catherine gamely on the shoulder, stood, and headed for the door.

"Sister?" Catherine asked tentatively. Julian pivoted back toward her. "I just noticed that small bit of paint peeling in the corner..." She couldn't help herself.

"No worries! I'll get it tomorrow!"

"Thank you so much." Catherine gave what she imagined was a sporty little wave as Julian headed for the door. "Good luck at the Nationals!" Julian nodded, smiled, and was gone.

Life simply could not be that uncomplicated, Catherine thought. Pickleball lines taped over the tennis court lines. The Nationals. She recalled the night several months ago when she'd heard a rhythmic whacking sound coming from the basement and gone to investigate. There was Julian, at 1:00 AM, hitting the hard plastic whiffleball against the basement wall, wearing red shorts and a yellow tee shirt. What would it be like, always knowing just what to do and where to put your feet?

A loud rap on the doorjamb, and Mary Pat's face craned around from the corridor.

"Come in, Sister," Catherine said, beckoning her to the chair. Mary Pat strolled in twirling a black bead rosary on her index finger like a keychain. A small black presence trailed a few feet behind her, no longer held safely in Mary Pat's arms but apparently finding his own footing around the convent. Maybe Mary Pat figured that the new regime was a good time to bring Scat out of the closet. She fell into the chair and Scat bounded smoothly onto her lap, melting into her as if they were one being. Mary Pat reached over the cat and handed the rosary to Catherine.

"A little memento of your time here," she said with a wry smile, stroking Scat's back absentmindedly.

Had anyone here actually seen her say the rosary? No, because she hadn't done so. She chose to believe that Mary Pat had just wanted to give her a gift, and that the rosary was simply something she had at hand that might be appropriate for a nun, even a fake one. It was the thought that counted.

"Thank you. Very kind." She smiled and tucked the rosary into her pocket. Mary Pat continued to stare at her, but had stopped smiling. Okay, Catherine thought, no more small talk. "You know, I never understood what drew you here, or what you were looking for. And I don't know if you got it." She glanced at the peeling paint, then back at Mary Pat. "But I don't think you did."

Mary Pat emitted a small huff, turned sideways in the chair, and then back to face Catherine. "You're right. I didn't."

Catherine asked quietly, "What did you want?"

Mary Pat seemed to consider what to say, shrugged, and then blurted, "I wanted God. I wanted that feeling I read about, like the saints had. Like Yogananda and the swamis had. I wanted to feel God inside me. I tried. I spent more time on my knees than anyone when I was back in the real convent. A quarter century I did that, for nothing. Same thing out here, with all the conscious-raising and Eastern stuff. Drumming, for heaven's sake! Nothing! It was like Charlie Brown and the football. God was like Lucy, setting me up and then pulling it away, keeping it just out of reach. I guess I gave up. Then I heard about you guys, and figured it was as good a place as any to hide out. Three squares, enough freedom for my tastes, and I don't have to pretend to believe in anything. I'm pretty content here. Satisfied."

Catherine noticed that she had stopped breathing, and took a long, slow breath. Could someone want it that much and never get it? The strange thing was, Mary Pat didn't seem bitter. Just resigned.

"I'm so sorry," Catherine said gently. "I wish I'd... Is there anything I can do now?" She knew there wasn't. Not if Mary Pat had given up.

"Nah." Mary Pat shifted in her seat and now seemed antsy, as if she regretted having opened up. "Hey, don't worry about me. I'm fine." She started to stand, but Catherine pulled her gently back into the chair. She took the rosary out of her pocket and pressed it into Mary Pat's hand.

"Thank you for this, but I want you to keep it." She paused, feeling awkward. "Use it as a talisman. Of hope. Maybe you'll find what you're after." She felt inadequate, helpless, but didn't know what else to do or say.

"Sure. Thanks." Mary Pat gave her a perfunctory smile, stuffed the rosary into her pocket, tucked Scat under one arm, and ambled away. Catherine watched her go. Was God playing Lucy with her, too?

CHAOS AT THE NO NAME CONVENT · 203

The scent of sandalwood wafted into the dining room. Sister Heather was near! Catherine looked up to behold the former coven leader entering the dining room slowly, solemnly, holding before her at arm's length a little package wrapped in sparkling, crinkly crimson paper. She smiled enigmatically, swooped into the chair beside Catherine, and held out the little gift balanced precariously on her palms, "To see you on your sacred way, Sister Catherine."

Catherine gingerly picked the gift off Heather's hand platform, wondered briefly if there were something alive, or formerly alive, within its folds—Eye of newt? Toe of frog?—and asked tentatively, "Shall I open it now?" Heather leaned away and hooked her arm over the back of the chair.

"Of course! It's for you!" Then suddenly the quasi-mystical veil dropped and she seemed years younger. "You won't believe what it is!" There were times when Heather reminded her of Teresa. Maybe it was just their Valley-Girl-infused speech patterns, but they also had in common a careless way of walking on life without noticing where they were stepping. And despite their bravado, they both seemed a little afraid that they might fall through the surface and be lost.

Catherine carefully pulled back the wrapping. A small quartz crystal fell into in her right palm. It seemed alive! She wondered where it might have been.

"Amma blessed it!" Heather cried. "I had it in my hand when she hugged me, and I rubbed it across her shoulder!" This sounded vaguely familiar to Catherine, but she couldn't quite place who Amma was or why her blessing was such a big deal. She felt herself squint slightly.

"Amma?"

"The *hugging* saint?" Heather squealed.

"Ah yes! Amma!" Catherine nodded. The Indian woman who traveled the world, enlightening people with a hug. She held the crystal to her heart. "Thank you! This is wonderful."

"Just a little gift," Heather said casually. "Something to guide you in your new life."

"I'll treasure it," Catherine said, not knowing whether to slip the crystal into her pocket, put it back in the crinkly crimson paper, or just hold it. She settled on the latter and since Heather showed no signs of moving, began a conversation that would call on the little witch to talk and Catherine simply to listen. "I imagine you'll have quite a bit to contribute to the new workshops..."

"Oh!" Heather rolled her eyes and pantomimed exhaustion by laying her crossed arms on the table and burying her face in them, but quickly sat up again and launched into a full report. "I've just spent hours with Teresa. She'll need a lot of help. We'll start by cleaning out that Silicon Valley energy from her aura and..." Heather paused as if something in Catherine's demeanor—or her aura, Catherine speculated—had warned the former coven exec that she was going in the wrong direction. She continued less dramatically, focusing on her own role. "I'll be leading seminars on crystals, Gaia energy, herbs...you know. All that stuff's in my wheelhouse. I can do it all."

"And I'm sure you'll be very good at it." Heather looked up, looked down, and didn't seem to know what to do with herself. Catherine felt a hundred years old next to this wild, but somehow dear, little spinner. She took Heather's hands, looked into her eyes and tried to send the occult mistress all the peace and centeredness at her disposal, which wasn't much but was a lot more than Heather had. Tears formed in Heather's eyes.

"Thank you," she said, staring at Catherine and seeming more subdued than Catherine had ever seen her. "For everything." Catherine nodded and smiled, let go of Heather's hands. Heather stood and tossed over her shoulder as she glided out of the room, "Hey! Stop by Moonpath when you get up there. Tell them I sent you!"

"Of course! Thanks!" Catherine gave her a little wave, but Heather was already gone. The room seemed very quiet.

Outside, the sky was taking on amber tones. The wind was up, stirring in the Monterey pines across the street. It was 5:00 and the halls of the convent had emptied out. Catherine stood, a little stiffly, and sought out the chapel. From her regular seat in the back, she watched the shadows lengthen across the burnished pews. The reds became dark crimson, the greens turned to forest, the blues shifted slowly from sapphire to lapis. Where was Mary Margaret? Merged with the One? Doing a brief stint in Purgatory on her way to the Feet of God? She wished Mary Margaret were sitting next to her, taking her hand, telling her that everything would be all right even though she didn't have a mission in life and didn't even know what was next.

After a while, she heard footsteps in the hall and snatches of excited conversations. Driven partly by curiosity, partly by a need to keep to the routine since everything seemed up in the air, she rose and headed for the dining room.

*

Teresa met her at the door and guided her to the head of the table. "Our dear Sister Catherine will take her leave early tomorrow morning," she began, standing next to Catherine and sounding about ten years older than she had the day before. "I thought we might take this time, before we begin dinner, to thank her and remember our special times with her."

An awkward silence followed, and then they all seemed to want to talk at once. They were very kind, Catherine thought. Julian recalled the time she took Catherine to an A's baseball game in Oakland and Catherine spilled mustard from her hot dog all over her jacket. Jeanne brought in a freshly baked sourdough round "for the road tomorrow." Gemma thanked her for her guidance over the years. Mary Pat recalled Catherine's kindness to Scat, allowing the cat to become part of convent life even though she was "obviously not a cat person." Heather remarked that Catherine sometimes made her think of "the goddess" and stood as a reminder to her to stay on the sacred path.

Jeanne brought out mushroom, spinach, and onion quiche with a side of steamed broccoli, and they dug in. Catherine looked out over the group and thought that the conversation seemed livelier, the laughter more frequent and spontaneous, than it had been in quite a while. The air had cleared. The new order was in place. All that was left was for everyone to find her place in it. She would miss these women.

For dessert, Jeanne brought out a large chocolate sheet cake with "Thank you, Sister Catherine" written across it in pink buttercream and tiny purple OM symbols in each corner.

"A toast to Sister Catherine," Teresa called out, standing and raising a glass of water. They all stood and raised their glasses.

"Sister Catherine!" they called out.

"Speech!" Mary Pat demanded. "Speech!"

Catherine stood and motioned them into their seats.

"Thank you. Thank you so much. For all of this, and for your kind words. I will miss you very much. More than you know." She paused and stood up straighter. "The road ahead for me seems a little uncertain tonight." She looked around and saw concern on their faces. "Perhaps we're all embarking on a path through the unknown. That's uncomfortable, but I think it's good for us!" Smiles. Reassurance. "It makes us grow, and feel the Divine more deeply. You will be in my prayers as you open into that new path, and I hope I'll be in yours." She paused, and couldn't think of anything else to say. "Now please, finish this delicious cake!"

They stayed late in the dining room that night, and came in twos and threes to sit with her. She felt like one of them. Not the prioress, but a sister.

Finally, people started drifting away. Catherine headed up the stairs—one of the last times she would put her feet on these old tiles, she realized—and started packing. There wasn't much to pack. A few clothes, some books, her computer. It would all fit into a roller bag and a large backpack. She hung her aubergine robe carefully in the closet. Should she take it with her? It would be a memento of this time in her life, the ten years she had spent building and nurturing this place. She should have a talisman to represent that she had done something valuable, something substantial—and to remind her who she was. But she wasn't that person anymore, and she knew that she would be tempted enough to wallow in the past, to relive moments, to let her mind drift back to a former life that no longer existed. The robe would stay here. Jeanne would know what to do with it. That night, she slept more deeply than she had in years.

She had planned to sneak away at 5:30 the next morning, but found Teresa and Gemma waiting for her at the foot of the stairs. It dawned on her that losing these two women would be like losing parts of herself. Each of them seemed to sense that a hug was better than talk. Finally, Gemma said, "Safe trip. Drive carefully."

Tears rolled down Teresa's cheeks. "I'll miss you!"

Catherine put a hand on her shoulder, then lifted her roller bag into the trunk and tried to smile as she waved and drove away.

CHAPTER SEVENTEEN

THE NEW LAND

Three blocks from the convent, Catherine pulled over to the side of the road. She leaned her forehead on the steering wheel, made herself take a deep breath, and let the tears come. It was over. Waves of grief washed over her, laced with fear, humiliation, and just a drop of relief.

Finally, the tears exhausted themselves. She leaned back and watched the traffic whizz past her. Should she really go up to Sonoma? It had been a good story to tell the others and she liked the place, but she could go anywhere she wanted. What about Santa Cruz? She recalled a hot, sunny day, pre-convent, when she and some friends had drunk beer and eaten deep fried artichoke hearts on the Santa Cruz Beach Boardwalk, then driven north and dropped acid at the beach. Or Mendocino with its soft, loamy redwood forests, quaint little eateries, and youthful dope harvesters wandering the tiny tourist town with dazed expressions. Neither seemed right. For now, Sonoma was better. She knew the territory a little. Knew where to find fresh-picked cherries and an extravagant buttery pastry. She could get her feet on the ground up there. Figure out who she was, or who she wanted to be now.

She fished around in the glove box for something to dry her tears and found a McDonald's napkin from her recent visit. If she shook off this torpor and got moving, she promised herself, she could reprise that sumptuous runaway feast. She took another deliberate breath, edged out into traffic, and moments later was flying north under the orange-vermilion towers of the Golden Gate Bridge. In twenty minutes, she was hunkered over a Double Quarter Pounder, fries, and chocolate shake in the McDonald's parking lot and scoring a few more nights at Sally Abilene's Airbnb in Glen Ellen. She would hang out there, cry whatever tears needed to be cried, and scout for an apartment that could be her cocoon, a safe place in which to grow herself into whatever was next.

*

Catherine's cocoon turned out to be a small studio in a long, low apartment building that looked like a run-down motel just off busy Arnold Drive south of Glen Ellen. Dingy white walls, a small window facing the parking lot, and a thin, well-worn tan carpet. It was what she could afford. With a desk, futon, and chair from a thrift shop on the Sonoma Square, it was as fancy as her room at the convent had been, and a whole lot bigger. Anyway, she had things to do. Internal things like coming to terms with what had happened at the convent and what to do about herself now. External things like cranking out Lacy Dominion bodice-rippers at a record pace to give herself some wider housing options.

Each morning she made coffee, meditated as well as she could, wrote in her journal, and then became a highly energized, speed-typing Lacy Dominion. She was usually written out by early afternoon and headed up to Jack London Park just above Glen Ellen. Over the first six months, she started going beyond her usual hikes to Wolf House and the lake, and pushed out into Jack London's 29 miles of back-country trails lined with madrone, Douglas fir, black oak, buckeye, and bigleaf maple. She crossed golden grassy meadows and found 200-foot-tall redwoods, met squirrels and lizards, a few snakes, some coyotes, a fox, a bobcat, and once, in a clearing, a buck with an enormous rack of antlers. She discovered the Ancient Redwood, at least 2,000 years old, and sat in its presence for hours. Never in her life, even as a child, had she let herself just sit for that long without doing or producing something, or even thinking about anything in particular. The afternoon sun dappled through the redwoods and madrones, creating and recreating patterns on the ground and trees, and even in the redwood-dusted air as a gentle breeze came and went. The Ancient Redwood didn't speak, but it pulsed with her in a silence punctuated only by birdsong—towhees and warblers, finches, and hawks spiraling slowly above it all.

She hiked hundreds of miles in those first few months and found other places to sit, silent and still, letting the landscape of vineyards, meadows, forests, and wild flowers do their mysterious, mindless, wordless healing. Sally from the Airbnb was the only person she knew and Catherine hung out with her a bit, but mostly she was alone. She had a few insights—she'd been attached to an ego-driven role and paid the price, spiritual backsliding was inevitable unless you were passionately engaged ("Use it or lose it."), everything and everyone changes—but nothing particularly new or earthshaking. And yet something was different. She was still empty inside, but it was starting to feel like a good kind of empty.

After a year, Sally announced that she was going to spend eighteen months in Costa Rica deciding whether or not to retire there, and asked Catherine if she wanted to rent the house at a nominal fee and supervise the Airbnb unit in the back while she was gone. Catherine was delighted. The house was close to Jack London Park and had a big side porch where she could sit in the evening and watch the sun sink down behind the Sonoma Mountains. Inside, it was all homey wood and multicolored hooked rugs, with a big dark green sofa in front of a stone fireplace. It was a huge step up from the shabby apartment on Arnold Drive and felt like a soft, beautiful shawl around her shoulders.

She didn't know much more about herself or her direction than she had when she arrived from San Francisco, but she had stopped hurting so much, no longer felt so embarrassed by what had happened back at the convent, and had stopped worrying about wasting time when she just sat still. When she listed those accomplishments in her journal, she didn't think they amounted to much. But she could feel herself slowly becoming a different person from the speedy *faux* nun who had flown over the bridge just twelve months earlier—and that was a good thing.

*

At Sally's house, Catherine settled back into the daily routine. Coffee, journaling, pumping out Lacy books to the delight of her publisher, and afternoon walks in nature. She went even farther afield, traveled higher on the mountain, and spent more time just sitting quietly on a rock, a fence, or even a downed log. She still had to fight the occasional urge to jump up and at least cover a few more miles, but she was getting more comfortable with simply soaking in the warm, heavy air that always carried a slight scent of sulfur from the surrounding hot springs. She absorbed the sights and sounds of fir-covered mountains and lush redwood forests. Opened into the songs of doves, the rattling of woodpeckers, and the reeling of hawks and turkey buzzards in slow spirals above her. Everything seemed utterly still in those moments. And yet she knew that mice and gophers, lizards and tiny birds were skittering around in the bushes and ground cover, that the leaves were doing their thing with sunlight, and that life was surging even in the silence.

When she got very still, it seemed like even the air around her was a living thing, a presence that held her and permeated her. Her mind went utterly blank and she found herself...happy. For no reason. That easy happiness was simply what flooded in when everything else was quiet. It wasn't the overwhelming high of the *samadhis* in India, which made her feel like she was being transported into other realms. It was just a soft, friendly kind of happy. At first, she had tried to goad it into a thundering *samadhi*. But that had only made her feel cranky and tired, so she gave it up.

She wondered about those thundering *samadhis*, and about a spiritual journey focused exclusively on attaining them. She wondered about all the mental constructs of the Divine, from the Church's bearded old white man on the cloud, to the mystics' blissful All Is One, to the idea that everything seen and unseen is just conscious energy swirling around without any particular values or purpose. In the end, she gave up wondering and told herself that, by definition, whatever the Divine was could not be fathomed by the human mind. She had spent a lot of energy trying to nail it down and box it, and look where that had gotten her.

When she got back from walks, she sometimes collapsed onto the green sofa and took a nap before dinner. Taking naps felt like a weakness at first but, really, who would know? And if they did know, who would care? Nobody here expected her to be the straight-standing, commanding prioress in the aubergine robe, hypervigilant about what she and everyone else was doing, thinking, and saying.

In fact, she wrote in her journal that the prioress's studied, imposing presence might actually have been part of the problem. Her need never to waste time or energy, to see herself and be seen by others as powerful, focused, always striding toward the horizon...What good had that done anybody? Certainly, it hadn't done *her* much good. She'd thought that her spiritual slippage stemmed from being lazy, but maybe it was just the opposite. Maybe she'd been working too hard to duplicate the experiences she'd had in India, trying to jam something from the past into current reality, a square peg into a round hole.

Soaking in nature and silence was better, she decided, however decadent it felt. Just because it made her happy, didn't mean it was cheating.

*

As she hiked around the park, Catherine noticed several workers who were only there a couple of days a week. They didn't wear uniforms, and seemed more like friendly neighbors than authoritative park employees. They groomed trails and tended gardens. They collected fees and answered questions at the little welcome kiosk at the park entrance, sold souvenirs at the small museum, even led tours for visitors. They all seemed to know one another and be rooted to the park, or to the town, or to something that connected them. She felt shy about intruding on their common ground, so never approached them with anything more than a "Hi" or "Nice day." The idea of being a newcomer in a whole new group seemed overwhelming. What if they asked her where she had come from? Or what she did for a living?

One afternoon, returning from a long hike on the Mountain Trail, she spotted a lone woman kneeling in the garden near the trailhead. Weeding? She wore a pink baseball cap with a long grey-blonde ponytail sticking out the back, baggy jeans, and a denim shirt with the sleeves rolled up. After a minute, she stood up a little stiffly and took a swig of water, looked Catherine's way and waved. The woman appeared to be friendly, she was alone, and it seemed like the perfect opportunity to find out about those people. Catherine waved back and started down toward the garden.

"Hi," the woman said, extending her hand. Her face was tanned, with lots of smile lines and bright blue eyes. "I'm Joan Halliday. I've seen you before. You hike a lot."

Catherine couldn't remember the last time she had felt tongue-tied. "Catherine Walsh. I moved up from the city a little over a year ago. It's so beautiful here." Joan nodded.

"You're staying at Sally's?" Holy shit! How did she know that? "Small town," Joan said apologetically. A list of other things that people might know about her raced through Catherine's mind, but she tried to keep a neutral expression.

"Sally's in Costa Rica," she said. "But you probably know that."

Joan smiled knowingly. "She won't be able to stand the quiet. She'll be back." That took Catherine by surprise. Sally had seemed so excited about Costa Rica. If she came back and reclaimed the house, where would Catherine stay?

"Do you work for the park?"

Joan laughed, "Oh no! Volunteer. Almost everybody here's a volunteer! You should do it! It's fun, and you get to know people."

"I'd like that," she heard herself say. But now that the possibility of meeting people was actually opening up, she had a moment of pause. Was she ready for that much change?

"Come up to the museum with me and meet Rick. He's in charge of volunteers. Almost anything you want to do here, he'll make it a volunteer job for you."

Catherine started to say how busy she was, but didn't. She was already trying to decide between collecting day fees at the kiosk and leading visitor tours.

"Okay. Thank you!"

On the ten-minute walk to the museum, they exchanged getting-to-know-you information. Joan's husband had died two years earlier. She had two grown children, three grandchildren. Worked four days a week at the bead store on the Sonoma Square, and the other three up here. She had only read one of Jack London's books and didn't like it, but had been in love with the park for decades. She sewed, cooked, lifted weights, and was taking her grandkids to a dude ranch in Montana the next summer. Catherine divulged more information than she had shared with another human being in decades. She astonished herself by giving an accurate description of her last ten years and even a somewhat watered-down account of what had happened when Teresa took over the convent. Amazingly, she was still standing when they arrived at the museum. And she felt fantastic. Joan seemed not so much horrified or appalled as intrigued and even a little impressed.

Rick was a tall, quiet, sandy-haired guy about 60 with a slow, even smile and a gentle way. He signed her up to work at the welcome kiosk two afternoons a week. As she and Joan walked back to the garden, Catherine said, "I can't believe I did that!"

Joan acted as if signing up to volunteer were a natural part of life. "Oh, you'll love it. You'll like the other folks. And now you'll have a pass!"

The compensation for volunteering was a free pass to the park. Catherine had already bought the annual $50 pass, but the free pass somehow made her part of the community. Not exactly one of the gang, perhaps, but more respectable and official than she had been a half hour earlier.

She and Joan exchanged contact info and Joan said, "Hey, I'm having a game night on Saturday. Can you come?" A room full of people playing board games, cards, maybe even charades. People who would know her only as the strange hiking woman "staying at Sally's."

"Sure! Thanks! And thanks for all this, Joan."

Walking back to Sally's, Catherine panicked about what to wear to the game night. She had no idea what would be appropriate, and didn't want to ask. After a few frantic moments of mentally scanning all her clothes and rejecting each item, she circled back and found Joan still digging in the garden. She felt about eight years old.

Joan looked up with a smile. "Hey!"

Catherine knelt down beside her and stared at the weeds. "Um. What's the dress for Saturday? I'm new and…" Joan acted as if this were a perfectly normal question.

"Oh, just clean jeans. Very informal. I ask people to take off their shoes, so…"

"Thanks." Catherine gave her a grateful smile as she stood and headed back to Sally's. She would have to buy some new socks.

*

On game night, Catherine stared down at the three pair of newly purchased socks lined up on her bed: dark red, dark blue, and beige with a pattern of fir trees. Each carried about twenty pros and twenty cons, and she was no closer to a decision than she had been in the store. The fir trees were her favorite, but she thought they might be seen as attention-seeking. She snapped up the red ones, pulled them on, and checked the mirror once more. Clean jeans per Joan's instructions, a crisp white blouse, some Burt's Bees lip gloss, and her hair in the ponytail that the older women of Glen Ellen seemed to favor. Not too dressed up, but a little more put together than the woman they had seen on the trails. It would have to do.

Joan met her at the door with a hug and called out to the fifteen or so people milling around behind her, "Hey everyone! It's Catherine! The *nun!*" Screams of delight from a few of the women, grunts of approval from the men, and six or seven of them surged forward to shake hands and introduce themselves. Well, she wouldn't have to worry about them finding out where she'd spent the past ten years. They probably knew the whole story, Teresa and all.

"Red or white?" asked Bill, who looked like a TV lawyer and carried a bottle of red wine in one hand, white in the other. He turned out to be Joan's rather casual boyfriend, which was to say that when and if either of them thought it might be nice to go on a date, they called one another.

"Water's good," Catherine smiled back at him. Knowing nods from several of them. The AA crowd, she figured. Rick, the volunteer guy, waved at her from the corner and she waved back, glad to recognize someone other than Joan.

"Come with me," Mike urged, taking her elbow and guiding her toward a card table. "We need a fourth for Pictionary!" He was about fifty, short but solid, with a full head of bright red hair and an infectious smile. At the Pictionary table, he introduced her to Lucy and Rob.

Without even trying, she was swept up into the group. Most of them were about her age. A few kids, a few older folks. About half men, half women, but they didn't seem particularly coupled up. Maybe game night was just for the unattached. She played Pictionary, pinochle, and Charades and laughed more than she had in a long time. At about 10:00, the tables were taken down and the games put away. Everybody gathered around the fireplace in chairs, sofas, and pillows on the floor, and chatted over another glass of wine.

At one point Mike stood, raised his glass, and said, "To Catherine, our #1 Pictionary player tonight. Welcome! Come again next month!" A round of applause and then Joan, who was a little tipsy, piped up, "Hey, I forgot to ask what you do! Sally's not letting you stay for free, I bet!" Guffaws, probably at Sally's expense.

Well, in for a penny...

"Ever heard of Lacy Dominion?"

CHAPTER EIGHTEEN

KINTSUGI

Catherine loved working at the kiosk. Greeting people, answering their questions, and handing out maps and hiking advice made her feel as if she were giving them a gift, and also giving back to the park in some way. She started hiking with some of the game night gang, but only once or twice a week. She needed her time alone on the trails to stay steady and nurtured. She also had to keep up the flow of Lacy Dominion books, but that was happening without much effort. And Lacy's heroines were getting their bodices ripped less frequently, and embarking on seafaring adventures of their own more often.

Late one night, she sat on the green sofa staring into the fire, reflecting on all that she had un-become since arriving in Glen Ellen. She looked up at Sally's beautiful blue ceramic bowl on the mantle. Sally had made it herself at a class in town, and loved to tell the story of how she had created the stunning swirls of indigo, royal blue, peacock, and teal. Catherine thought it was exquisite, and had moved it from the kitchen to the mantle to make it more visible, honor it, and keep it safe.

That blue bowl felt like a touchstone for her journey, with the swirls being all the ups and downs of the past year. She still awoke with a start some nights, awash in shame that the whole convent had turned against her and worried that she might be wasting her life now, sinking into inertia, hiding out in the country where no one could see her, writing books about wild women because she herself had become so unwild, "relaxing" into torpor and abandoning any hope of improving herself.

But then the sun would come up and light would splash over the Valley. She would take a cup of coffee out onto the deck, sit listening to the little birds, watch life wake up, and remember that even though she didn't have a map of the trail she was on, she had become more sure-footed and better at intuiting the right turns. So what if she didn't let herself think about Teresa, Gemma, Mary Margaret, and the rest of them? So what if she avoided the city? She was good up here, and learning to hike without a map. She glanced up at the blue bowl and wondered if those swirls might be some sort of secret map.

The fire was almost out and she was tired. She pulled herself up off the sofa and leaned a hand on the mantle as she stooped to bank the coals. A loud crash split the air! She looked down at the tile floor and saw the blue bowl shattered into pieces. Six! No, seven pieces! She gathered up the shards in a panic. How could she have done that? Sally's prize possession. It was so beautiful! Had *been* so beautiful! Blood seeped from two of her fingers. She ran to the kitchen, grabbed a thick towel, and carefully laid out the pieces. Ran her fingers under the faucet. The cuts weren't deep, so she wrapped them in paper towel for the moment. She stared, horrified, at the jagged blue pieces laid out on the white towel, set off by smears of her own dark red blood.

She tried fitting the pieces together to see if she had all of them—first in her mind, and then actually picking them up and matching the edges. It looked like they were all there, but she ran back to the couch and looked all over the floor for small pieces just in case. There were none, so she headed back to the kitchen. The breaks appeared to have been clean. Elmer's glue? No. She googled how to fix ruined ceramic bowls and found all sorts of solutions, most involving epoxy, multiple syringes, and toxic items that she didn't have on hand and clearly couldn't have mastered in her present state even if she'd had them. This was a job for the morning.

She placed another towel over the shards and headed for the bathroom to bandage her fingers. So she wasn't in such great shape after all. Or had started to get there and sabotaged herself. Sally's dazzling hand-made bowl, her own talisman for a new life. She took a Benadryl but still lay awake for an hour, staring at the ceiling and wondering if maybe she should have stuck it out at the convent.

*

In the morning, she surveyed the damage. It looked like all the pieces would fit together, but the elegant blue bowl would never be the same. She didn't trust the internet's solutions and instead decided to bring the problem to Jack, who owned the ceramics shop on the Sonoma Square. Maybe he could even do the repair himself!

Jack and his husband Ed were older guys, refugees from the city who no longer had to make money and so could do whatever they wanted with their shop, The Mystical Garden. They filled it with expensive ceramics and pottery, outré garden decorations, fancy candles, whimsical fabric dolls, hand-painted scarves, and delicate little figurines. Jack was a game night regular, dapper that morning in a crisp pink cotton shirt and plaid bow tie. He emerged from the back of the shop with open arms.

"Darling!" He stopped, touched the large paper bag she carried, and met her eyes. "What's wrong?" Catherine held back the tears and pointed to the bag. He led her to a counter near the back and took the bag from her, casting worried looks in her direction every few seconds. "What do we have here?" he asked. She had wrapped the shards in three towels, being careful to protect all the edges. Very deliberately, Jack began to extract each piece and lay it on one of the towels.

"It's Sally's bowl. She made it! I broke it! Can you fix it?"

He eyed her over his granny glasses, then focused on the shards. "Let's see what's going on." He examined each piece, laying it back on the towel, delicately fitting a few of them together. Not letting them touch, but seeing where the pieces would meet. Finally, he stood up straight, cocked his head to one side, and looked at her.

"I have an idea."

"But can you fix it?"

He reached over and patted her arm. "It's going to be alright. Have you ever heard of *kintsugi*?"

She looked at him as if he were insane. "No."

"It's a Japanese thing. When a bowl or cup, or anything, breaks into pieces, they glue the pieces back together with a lacquer dusted in fine metals like gold. Those gold seams are meant to show. They create beautiful, shining designs on the bowl, which then becomes a whole new entity. The point is that the bowl has been *through* something, faced a problem and turned it to the good—which makes it even more gorgeous! It's been broken, but the places where it's been broken are even stronger now, and more attractive. It's all about embracing impermanence and imperfection. Highlighting the break makes it worth more, personally and..." he raised an eyebrow, "sometimes even financially."

Catherine was skeptical. But it did make a certain sense, and she started warming to the idea.

"Could you do that?" she asked. He stepped back and folded his arms.

"No. But you could. It's not my break."

"I'm not an artist. I'm clumsy. I can't do crafts."

"This isn't a craft. It's a ceremony."

"I'll mess it up and make it even worse."

He eyed the pieces of ceramic on the counter. "Worse than this?" They both stared down at the shards. "They sell kits for this, you know. I could get you one. You could see how they do it on youtube. And, of course...practice, practice, practice." She could feel the tears coming again. "It'll make you feel better," he said quickly.

She might be a self-saboteur and a life-waster, but she was not stupid and this was not her first spiritual rodeo. When messages came that clearly, you just said, "Yes, boss."

*

Catherine spread Friday's edition of the newspaper over the long wooden dining room table and arranged her tools in a row. The *kintsugi* kit Jack had gotten for her contained a double-barreled syringe of epoxy, some powdery gold mica, a dish in which to mix the two, several pieces of wood that looked like ultra-skinny popsicle sticks, surgical gloves, and a sheet of instructions—which she had already read four times. She eyed the epoxy warily. She didn't understand it, and didn't like it. It seemed to want to stick her fingers together, or poison her with its fumes, or in some way make her fail at the *kintsugi* process. But really, she just had to mix it up with the gold mica—and after that, how hard could the rest of it be?

Jack had insisted that she take a broken teacup from the shop, ivory with a pink and green floral pattern, and practice on it. But she couldn't imagine getting through this process once, let alone twice. Besides, she had watched a youtube video three times and that should count as practice. Jonathan, the youtube *kintsugi* instructor, was a younger version of Jack with a crew cut and a smooth, mellifluous voice. He casually mixed up the epoxy and mica, deftly scooped up a bit of it on a wooden stick, applied it to one edge of a broken black cup, and slowly, magically, pressed the other half of the cup to the seam. A perfectly even line of lustrous gold oozed forth from the place where the cup has been broken. He warned viewers to do only two pieces at a time, let them set for five minutes, and then continue to add shards one by one until they held in their hands "a fabulous item, veined with glorious gold."

Jonathan had seemed overly encouraging, overly solicitous, almost to the point of being smarmy—but now she realized that his viewers probably needed that extra dose of comfort. Like herself, they were probably undone by having broken the item in the first place, and further undone by the prospect of now having to create something even more beautiful than the original. With epoxy! They probably weren't breathing, either. At the end of the video, Jonathan had lowered his voice to a conspiratorial near-whisper and advised the newly-minted *kintsugi* masters to mix only small amounts of epoxy and mica at a time because it hardened very quickly.

Catherine arranged the pieces of the blue bowl on the table and stared at them a moment, deciding which two to join first. She felt herself getting a little faint, a little disembodied, and forced a deep breath. She squeezed a small amount of epoxy into the dish, spooned in a tiny bit of mica, and stirred. Immediately, swirls of light, medium, and dark gold appeared, sparkling in the light from the overhead lamp. With trembling hands, she picked up a skinny popsicle stick in one hand and a blue shard in the other, dipped the stick into the thick, shining liquid, and applied it to the broken edge. Then placed the matching shard against it. Sure enough, just as Jonathan had promised, gold material oozed from the seam. You had to hold the two pieces together for five minutes so they would set, but her hands were still shaking and the line of gold was getting a bit ragged. She put her elbows on the table to steady her hands, which jostled the two edges apart briefly. She smooshed them back together quickly, which made the gold line even more jagged, but was able to stay relatively still for the remainder of the setting time. When she placed the two joined pieces on the table, her gold line didn't look anything like Jonathan's. There was a big glob at one end, and an uneven smear at the other. How had she done that? Why hadn't she practiced? Now she'd ruined the "fix."

She grabbed the next shard of blue bowl and tried scooping some gold onto the wooden stick, but the epoxy on the stick had already hardened into a misshapen bulb and the stuff in the dish was nearly solid. Why hadn't they included another dish!? She ran to the kitchen for some heavy-duty aluminum foil to use as a substitute dish. Squeezed epoxy onto it, added the mica, grabbed another popsicle stick, and began applying gold to one edge of the shard. She willed her hands to stop shaking. She would master this and make it work! The line was a little better. Not much, but some. But as she started to let go, the two pieces began to fall apart. She had to slam them back together or lose the whole thing. The resulting gold line was not exactly a line. There was one original vein, some smearing, and another random thread of gold on top of it all.

She never should have started this—but now that she had, she had to keep going. She had *told* Jack she was no good at crafts. But wait, he had said it wasn't a craft. It was a ceremony. She couldn't imagine what kind of ceremony could rise out of the mess on this table. To distract herself, she looked out the glass slider to Sonoma Mountain in the distance, watched some little wrens scurry about on the deck, let the eucalyptus in the side yard take hold of her and calm her. She looked back at the remaining shards and decided to treat them gently. Trying to make them do her will certainly wasn't working. She would just do it however she did it, and the outcome would be whatever it was.

She mixed up more epoxy and mica on the aluminum foil and picked up the next shard. Smoothed on the gold, held the edges together, and breathed into the five-minute wait. It looked good. She placed it back on the table and, just to make sure, took off her right glove and touched the line. It gave way! Not completely set! The pieces held together but a small fingerprint appeared on the shiny vein. Okay…okay, she told herself. Not the end of the world.

Three shards left. She put the glove back on, picked up the next piece, and applied the gold slowly and carefully, just as Jonathan had done. As if it were easy, even fun. It looked almost as good as his! Not quite. But not like her early attempts. For the next shard, she emptied her mind and let the gold go wherever it wanted to go. Also good. The gold was wise. As she spread gold along the final shard, the material seemed to reach up to her, smile, and relax into a perfect line.

The bowl was a bowl again! She placed it on a clean piece of newspaper at the end of the table and stood back to take it in. Some nice, even gold lines against the dark blue. Some jagged ones, some lumpy ones, and a few smears. She didn't know whether or not it was beautiful, but she liked the way it looked. It would need to cure for a couple days, and so would she. As she was cleaning up, she realized that she'd forgotten all about the ceremony! Then she remembered gazing out the window. Maybe ceremonies didn't always look the way she thought they should.

A week later, Sally called from Costa Rica. She loved the place even more than she'd anticipated. She had made friends and a new life there, and wasn't waiting for retirement to move. She wasn't coming back at all, asked Catherine to keep, give away, or sell most of what she'd left in Glen Ellen, and offered to sell Catherine the house at a very reasonable price. Catherine swallowed hard and accepted. That night, she put the bowl back on the mantel. It was in the place of honor again, but it looked quite different. Richer, more lustrous. And hers.

*

Three years after she arrived in Glen Ellen, Catherine sat looking out at the sunset from her deck. Tangerine, lavender, and gold streaked the horizon. Amber light fell on Shakti's grey muzzle, resting on her lap. She had never had a pet, but an adopted senior Golden Retriever turned out to be the perfect companion. And today had been a perfect day. She had written for hours about Lacy Dominion's latest heroine, who was setting sail for the New World. Then she and Shakti hiked up to the Ancient Redwood. Afterward, she drove into town, bought some chocolate-dipped palmiers, and took them over to Jack's shop to eat with their coffee. Then home to grill wild salmon and asparagus with Joan. Now she and Shakti were settled in to enjoy the quiet of the evening.

Something about the day, and the peace she felt out on the deck, gave her the courage to google "No Name Convent" for the first time since leaving San Francisco. Up popped a slick site with a big header that alternated among a wide shot of the elegant little chapel; a group shot of Teresa, Gemma, Jeanne, and two other women she didn't recognize grinning into the camera; and the convent's newly renovated exterior—a strange amalgam of art deco and India, not unlike the Ananda Center. They must be doing well. She clicked on the "Offerings" tab and found twelve different courses and workshops, among them Jeanne's "Holiness of Housework" which was given once a month and appeared to be very popular; Gemma's meditation classes; Teresa's "Spirituality of Leadership" course; a variety of yoga, tai chi, and massage workshops; and "Pickleball and the Kingdom" taught by Julian. The No Name had found a place even for her, and she had obviously found something that kept her there, rather than traveling the world for tournaments.

Catherine clicked on the "Our Mission" tab and found:

The No Name Convent is dedicated to opening up our experience of the Divine in every aspect of life. We provide a supportive community for people to explore who they are, enhance their relationships with others, and unfold the godliness within themselves.

Sister Teresa, CEO

That's exactly what Mary Margaret had wanted! Catherine saw that if she had stayed at the convent, this never would have happened. Nor would she have become the person she was today, and she liked that person better than the prioress. She stroked Shakti's head and the dog nuzzled in. The sky was fading into purple with a few streaks of gold and crimson above the dark green mountain. She smiled as a quiet happiness wrapped itself around her.

Grace had found her, in spite of herself. She wasn't sure exactly where it had come from, or how it had spotted her out on the trails, just putting one foot in front of the other—but it was all she'd ever wanted.

ABOUT THE AUTHOR

Carol Costello lives in San Francisco.
Her other books include:

Chasing Grace: A Novel of Odd Redemption

Change or Die: A Novel of Spiritual Evolution

The Soul of Selling

www.carolcostello.net

Made in United States
Troutdale, OR
03/03/2024